What people are saying about Jenny Gardiner's books:

Red Hot Romeo

"Awesome". So enjoyed the romantic chemistry between the two characters. Read it non stop into the wee hours. Highly recommend this book
-- Mrs. K

Blue-Blooded Romeo

"Another brilliant, fun read from Jenny Gardiner. The book is fun to read and I thoroughly enjoyed every word. Jenny Gardiner has put the fun back into romance books and I look forward to each book in this delightful series."
-- Anne Blyth

"I had planned on only reading a few chapters at first but couldn't put it down. A terrific storyline, well-developed and extremely relatable characters, what's not to love?? Great read!"
-- Samantha Reeves

Falling

for

Mr. Maybe

(book two of the Falling for Mr. Wrong series)

by Jenny Gardiner

Chapter One

GEORGIA Childress took an odd sort of pride in all the dinks and rust spots her fifteen-year-old chalk-yellow Volvo station wagon sported. Maybe they weren't exactly badges of honor, but each one had its own little story to tell, even if they did occasionally remind her of some of her more blond moments while driving—when she could have paid more attention behind the wheel. And at the end of the day, it told a little bit of a story of who Georgie was, like it or not.

The good news is nothing all that bad ever happened during those episodes. Even the time she backed out erratically and scraped bumpers with the mayor (four-inch-long black streak on the front right bumper) ended up being okay; Mayor Petrilli liked Georgie enough to hire her to pet sit her two yellow Labs when she went on vacation for two weeks. Granted she did insist that she not take the dogs in her car, but nevertheless, it was all good.

And that time she backed into her best friend's brother Max's ten-speed bike (ten-inch scrape caused by the bike's hand brakes along the center of the trunk), it worked out. Yeah, it did cost her a few hundred dollars in bike repairs, but he didn't stay mad at her. At least not for long.

Georgie had just gotten back into her car after taking a

late-day stroll along the beach. Whenever she had a chance to take a break and sink her toes into the warm, fine sand along the shoreline, she did so. It was her happy place, listening to the repetitive swoosh of waves upon the shore, the persistent cawing of seagulls swooping for fish. Walking along the beach helped her put life into perspective and gave her a sense of inner peace.

Summer was on the wane, and soon the beach landscape would take on an entirely different complexion and not be so welcoming to bare feet and tank tops. Although Georgie was happy to stroll beachside even with snow falling from the sky—unfortunately becoming rarer here in North Carolina—she was happiest on a day like today. Wisps of cotton candy clouds laced the late-afternoon sky as the sun cast its warm melon glow across the sand.

It's one of the reasons she moved back to Verity Beach in the first place. Something about the ocean called to her. She loved the ocean so much, she sometimes swore she must have been a mermaid (better that than, say, a sea manatee or a man-of-war jellyfish) in a past life. Although, yeah, that whole broken engagement in DC thing certainly impelled her homeward as well. Nothing like being dumped weeks before your marriage to the man you thought loved you to send you scurrying back to a place of comfort and familiarity.

Georgie knocked the sand off her feet and slid them back into her flip-flops. She needed to get to the grocery store and pick up something to make for dinner, and it was getting late. Her tummy was rumbling and she freely admitted she was a slave to that demanding organ.

She put the key in the ignition, switched the radio to her favorite station, and threw the car in reverse, accelerating out of her space maybe a little faster than necessary. Until she heard a loud crunch and slammed on the brakes.

"Crap," she said, throwing open her door—and dinging a half-inch mark in the car door next to hers in the process—as she walked to the back to see what happened.

She scrunched up her chin and pursed her lips as she took in the sight. A surfboard was lopped in half, one side partially dangling by some strands of wood but hanging at a perpendicular angle to the other half of it, which seemed to have smushed into the back end of the car next to her, leaving an ugly dent in the vehicle.

Which was evidently owned by a cute guy with a huge scowl on his face.

"Hey lady," he shouted, shaking his fist. "What the fuck? You murdered my board!"

Georgie knew that was her cue to apologize profusely, even as she stared at the guy, whose wet suit was stripped down to his lean hips, exposing a beautiful, tanned chest with strong pecs, dusted with golden hair that complemented the dirty blond hair on his head and the sexy needs-a-shave scruff on his handsome face. He stood before her in bare, sandy feet. She loved sand-covered bare feet on a man.

"Oh my God, I am soooo sorry," Georgie said, reaching to lift the surfboard as if she could force the two pieces back together. She could not. "I don't know how I missed seeing that."

He was nodding his head as if in a catatonic state while flailing his arms in a fit of pique. "Any more than you could have missed an atom bomb dropping and the commensurate mushroom cloud," he said, his golden-hazel eyes wide with what might have been incredulity. "I mean what about the damned board could you not have seen when you were backing out? It's six freaking feet long. That's like not seeing a football team in your rearview mirror."

Georgie knit her brow, mortified but also indignant because it was as if he thought she'd done it on purpose.

"Except this was sideways, not up and down." She shifted her hands in a horizontal then vertical manner to demonstrate.

He cocked his head as if he was trying to grasp if she'd actually said that. She liked his hair: dirty blond and a little long, like he was about two months late for a haircut. The bottom edge of his hair curled up around his neck in a way that simply asked for you to run your fingers through it to smooth it out a bit. He wore a leather strand around his neck and a shark tooth was suspended from it. Lucky tooth to be located so close to his sexy chest.

"I'm not going to dignify that daft reply with a response."

"Look, again, I'm so very sorry," she said. "I don't know how I missed it. I was backing up. There was a glare in my mirror, I think. The sun was reflecting off of something and it blinded me for a second, and then, I don't know, your car was back there and it was at a weird angle I guess, and shit, look what I did to that too." Georgie nodded at the damaged car.

She grabbed her purse from the car and quickly whipped out a checkbook. "Perhaps I can write you a check and we can *not* report this to my insurance? I don't know that I can afford another increase this year."

He sized up her car, which, much to her embarrassment, was downright riddled with pockmarks. It was the only time she didn't feel so great about all the dings.

"Gee, ya think?" he said.

She rifled through her bag for a pen. "Just tell me how much it'll be to replace it and well—" She licked her finger and tried to wipe away the marks on the back of his car, but she knew damned well they weren't tiny bumper marks but an actual dent. "Well, that too." She pointed at it. "Again, I feel bad about that. I don't know what happened."

He shook his head, and if she wasn't mistaken, he looked as though he was about to throw up. He had that green-around-the-gills appearance of someone so upset it was a distinct possibility. "You can't pay me enough."

She stopped and looked up, pen in hand at the ready. "Well, now, that's silly. What do you mean I can't pay you enough?"

"It's one of a kind," he said. "I made it myself."

Georgie blanched and her lip curled into a snarl. What were the chances? She couldn't plow into a run-of-the-mill Walmart-special surfboard. No. It had to be a bespoke one.

If that didn't beat it all.

"Well, crap," she said. "Now I feel even worse." Her eyes started to moisten, and damn if she didn't hate when she cried. She tried to wipe away the nascent tears with her shoulders, as if pretending she was itching something on her face. But the thing is, she was one of those criers. A big ugly messy one, once she got going. And sure enough, it was like her eyes were leaking, the tears started coming so fast. And with that came a couple of forlorn sobs so pitiful she was sure she sounded like a dying hyena.

She set her checkbook on the roof of the guy's car then dug back into her purse in search of a tissue and pulled out one with a clumped-up wad of chewing gum stuck to it. After she bunched the thing up, she blew her nose, taking care not to stick the still mint-scented gum to her nostrils.

"Here I was going to enjoy this lovely day and that sunset, and it was so beautiful, it reminded me of peppermint and Christmas and deliciousness and now—" She thrust her lower lip out as she looked at him, and he had that look that men sometimes get when they wish they could find an off switch for a woman but know that one doesn't exist: quizzical yet annoyed, all tinged with anger.

She hated that look; it reminded her of her father right before he would light off on her mother and scream and yell and pound his fists into the wall, sometimes so hard he put holes into the drywall. And that memory made her eyes water up even more, particularly because it evoked her parents' broken marriage, which then stirred up memories of her own marriage, which never happened, and the next thing she knew she was slumped against the bumper of her beat-up old station wagon, bawling her eyes out and this strange man with the broken surfboard was leaning over her trying to calm her down.

"Look, lady, don't worry about it," he said. "I'll figure it out."

Between sobs, she tried to speak. "But you made it. I can't even buy you another."

"It'll be fine," he said, awkwardly rubbing her hair as if she was an excitable poodle that needed to be calmed down. "I was going to make a new one anyway."

She stopped crying for a minute and gave him a hopeful smile, which contrasted mightily with her tearstained cheeks. She suspected she looked like a kid who'd shattered his mother's family heirloom vase into a thousand pieces only to have the mom say not to worry, she can glue it back together. "You were?"

He furrowed his brow as he glanced at his murdered surfboard. "Yeah, in fact that was what I was planning to start working on this week," he said. "This one was getting old. Worn out." He kicked his toe along the sandy pavement.

She looked to see if maybe he'd crossed his fingers.

"Are you sure?"

"Um, yeah. Yeah. Of course."

She used her shoulders to swipe at another tear, realizing too late that she didn't even have fabric from her tank top to catch the tears and snot, and they both streaked across her still-tanned shoulders in a most inelegant manner. Oooh, she must've been a sight for sore eyes.

"Well please, let me write a check so you can fix everything, okay?" Her fingers trembled as she scrawled out an amount on her check, not even bothering to ask his name, instead leaving that line blank. "If you need anything more, my phone number's there." She pointed at her check.

His eyebrows ski-sloped toward his nose. He did not look particularly happy.

"Yeah, sure," he said, shoving the check into a hip pocket of his trunks that were peeking out from beneath his wet suit. He leaned over and looked at her face intensely, making Georgie uncomfortable, like he thought she might be unstable enough to walk straight into the ocean and keep on going till she was completely submerged, never to be seen again. "You okay?"

Come to think of it, that wasn't such a bad idea. If she were part mermaid, this would be the time to prove it. But that wasn't her style. She was certainly not a quitter. Besides, she hated being the center of anyone's attention, and certainly not that of the man whose board she destroyed, so she shrugged it off, waving her hand dismissively. "Hey, the good news is"—she nodded toward the board—"that didn't happen out there." She pointed toward the ocean. "And it's not covered in your blood, right? Way better my little fender-bender did this than a shark bite. Amiright?" She cracked a grin as she tried to make light of the situation.

The bummer on top of everything else was that the yummy orzo lemon meatballs she had planned to make after she went to the grocery store were no longer going to be on the menu for dinner. She'd lost her appetite with all the drama. So much for that.

Instead she smoothed out the pout that threatened to freeze on her face, then cupped her hand in a tiny wave as she climbed back into her car, pulling away ever so carefully to avoid any more disasters.

Chapter Two

SPENCER Willoughby wasn't sure exactly what hit him, figuratively speaking. He knew for sure what had quite literally hit his board and his car—a beat-up, piece-of-shit vehicle driven by a whacked-out woman who somehow managed to make *him* feel bad that she'd trashed his Petie. Petie was his term of endearment for the cherished surfboard he'd crafted lovingly from his own two hands, the board he'd ridden twice daily for the past three years.

For a second, he tucked away his outrage to try to digest what had transpired. Sheesh, that was the weirdest thing he'd experienced in a long while. Crazy lady surfboard killer cries and makes him feel bad.

What the ever-loving hell?

He kept looking at Petie, his hands caressing the smooth edges, his eyes not wanting to make contact with the harshly fractured scene of the crime that only drove home the board's premature demise.

He wanted to cry. His plans for the afternoon had been so simple: all he'd wanted to do was take in a few nice waves at sunset on a glorious Indian summer day, have a couple of beers, and call it a night. But now, shit, now not only could he not surf today, he couldn't surf on the very board it had taken him months to make. That sucked massively.

There was one good piece of news: he was nearly finished with one he'd started working on awhile ago, although it was originally intended as a gift for his kid brother Nate for Christmas. He knew, deep down, it would be dickish of him to keep it for himself. But then again, it's not like his brother would use it in late December. Oh, hell, who was he kidding? Even Spencer would use it in late December. That's why God invented wet suits, right?

His mind kept going back to the crazy lady who was bawling in front of him only minutes ago. How weird was that? He was the one with the dead board yet there he was left comforting her as if in her hour of need. He scratched his head, wondering how that turn of events came about.

Also, he wondered why he kept thinking about those aquamarine eyes of hers. When they'd filled with tears, they reminded him of tropical tide pools, and something about them pulled him in, despite his anger. Or maybe it was that smoking rack she was sporting. She wasn't a small girl by any stretch, and her luscious breasts complemented her size quite well—the two perfectly sized globes tucked into that hot pink tank looked so right. Here he was pissed at that strange woman yet all he could think about was how much he'd love to get his hands on those things.

At least his priorities were straight.

He laughed at that thought.

Meanwhile the amount of the check she gave him was pretty insignificant. It wasn't going to cover the cost of replacement wood, let alone the time it would take him to craft another board, and certainly not the dent in the back end of his car. Good thing he could get his buddy Ben Montgomery to bang out the dent, maybe even do a little quickie paint touch-up. The car was old and beat-up anyhow, so that wasn't his primary concern. It was simply how the hell was he going to surf until he finished his next board? He'd gotten spoiled with his baby. Now he was going to have to go back to one of his old store-bought surfboards, which was a bummer. Ah well, he was nothing if not flexible. He'd simply have to deal with it.

He pulled the woman's check out of his hip pocket and read it, realizing he hadn't even learned her damn name. He squinted at the small print till he saw it: Georgia Childress. Huh. She looked like a Georgia. Tall and strong, built like she knew how to take care of her body. He liked a woman like that. He stared at her phone number, wondering if maybe he should write that down, just in case. It was weird, her giving him a check. Who even wrote checks in this day and age? She could've Venmo'd him the money.

He grabbed his phone from the console of his car and snapped a quick picture of the check, phone number and all. That way if anything came up, he'd know how to get hold of her. Although right now the only thing that seemed like it was coming up was becoming a bit too obvious pressing against the crotch of his wet suit. Seriously, thinking about her tits had done this to him? What guy gets his board killed, his car dented, and can only think about how he might be able to get into the pants of the perpetrator? He laughed. Scratch that—pretty much every guy he knew.

Scrubbing a hand over his day-oldish beard, he shook his head. He had to put those thoughts out of his mind immediately. After all, he didn't come here to get involved with a woman, ditzy or not. He came here to get away from responsibility in all forms, and, well, crap, usually hopping on his surfboard served to clear his mind from such emotional pollutants. Looked like today he was going to have to pretend this never happened because that seemed the easiest way to purge the hot blond surfboard killer from his besotted mind.

He took one more look at his broken board.

Good luck with that, he thought, shaking his head.

Why did he have the nagging feeling she was going to be harder to cleanse from his thoughts than the others were?

Chapter Three

GEORGIE felt awful. It was bad enough she'd banged into a stranger's car, but to destroy the man's handmade wooden surfboard, well, that was beyond the pale. How could she have done that? She wished she could make a new one for the guy, but she hadn't a clue about woodworking. Or surfboards. For that matter, she didn't even know who the man was. She should have gotten his contact information. She could have followed up. Apologized again. Maybe invited him over for an *I'm sorry I didn't mean to kill your surfboard* dinner. Although, under the circumstances, he probably wasn't up for fraternizing with her. And she could hardly blame him.

But she wanted to do something. Maybe she could make him a gift, like, say, knit a sweater. But since she was left-handed, she never did get the hang of knitting. Everyone who ever tried to teach her had thrown in their knitting needles after the first lesson. She wondered if she was the only leftie knitting school dropout out there. You know things are bad when your knitting teacher bails on you.

Well, to hell with them. She was a crafty sort of girl without that knitting skill. She made pretty candles. Even those sand art sculptures that you put cacti in. Although to be honest she hadn't made either of those since probably sixth grade, so maybe she would have to remove that from her crafting skills resume. She used to make those lanyards by the dozens. Then again, that was at summer camp when she was ten. Hmmm… What else could she make?

She hit the heel of her hand to her head. *Of course!* How could she have not thought of this right off the bat? She was a talented quilter. She'd made several quilts, the last of which was buried with her mother when she passed away three years ago. She'd thought about keeping the quilt to remember her mom by, but she wanted her mother to be comfortable wherever she was. What if she got cold? Georgie wanted her to be cozy and warm and pain free. Maybe her mother would better remember her if she had that quilt, wherever she was now.

Georgie didn't like to dwell on that whole concept of afterlife and such. She hated that her mother might be alone somewhere out there. She'd had a hard-enough time of it when she was alive, between Georgie's father's hot temper and the divorce and then when her mother got sick. She took a lot of comfort knowing that quilt was still with her mother somewhere.

The other quilts she'd made were little wall hangings, but she thought it would be weird to make the guy a quilted wall hanging. Unless maybe they had surfer-themed ones, which she doubted. So then would she make him a full-out quilt? For his bed? That seemed odd too, didn't it? Make a quilt for a complete stranger who probably hates you, not knowing what he likes, even what colors he likes. Not to mention what size bed he sleeps in.

Hmmm… The thought of that guy sleeping in a bed stirred things up down there—a bit surprising considering Dan pulled a runner right before their wedding. Ever since, she'd started to think she was downright dead below the waist. That's why this hint of a resurfacing libido was potentially encouraging. One could argue, how could it not be? Because dang, that surfer was pretty hot. She closed her eyes and thought about his tanned chest, the taut abdomen, and that strip of sandy-blond hair that started at his navel and disappeared into the damned wet suit at such an inopportune location. If only that Lycra or neoprene or whatever those things were made from had been a little lower... No doubt he had on some board shorts or something beneath it, though, so she wasn't going to get a peek at anything more, regardless.

She wondered: did he sleep in the altogether? After all, it had been awfully hot lately, so he probably did sleep naked. All. Night. Long. Sprawled across a queen-sized mattress—or was it a king?—the sheets barely draped across his hips so she could visualize those cut abs right where she'd slip her hand beneath the crisp, white bedding. The bedding that would tent as soon as she placed her hand on his torso.

Oh. God. She had to stop contemplating the surfer dude in the buff. First off, she was never going to see him again. Second, even if she did—to give him the quilt she decided she would make just in case—she certainly wasn't going to see him naked. With a little luck, maybe he'd at least be stripped down in the wet suit. She could always hope.

Chapter Four

SPENCER peeled off his wet suit, then chucked his beat-up board in the back of the garage, behind the recycling bin, covering it with a drop cloth that lay in a heap nearby, if only to block it from his sight line. Out of sight, out of mind was what he needed for now. Even though he was going to be continually reminded of the demise of his surfboard every time he headed out to the beach, he'd have to ride the wave of the seven stages of grief. Maybe someday he'd be good with it. After all, he'd already breezed through shock and denial, limped through pain, steeped in guilt for not watching out for stupid drivers, trotted on past anger and bargaining, and slipped right on into depression. So that was four stages down in a matter of hours. He could do this.

But not without a couple of beers. He reached for his phone and called Ben, his good friend and surfside soothsayer, a name Spence gave him because he was so wise. More like a wiseass, but either way, it was all good.

"Dude. Beer. Now. Rooftop." Spencer never locked his door, so he knew Ben would come right on in. He stretched and scratched his chest as he walked to the refrigerator and grabbed a six-pack and an opener. He opened the sliding glass door, went out on the balcony, then climbed the stairs around the corner to the top of his beach house, which fronted a wide stretch of Carolina sand and overlooked the same waters that gave him his sanity.

The view alone was worth shaking up his life and taking off for the beach a few years ago, even if it did piss off his father and leave his mother behind wringing her hands in dismay. To steal a line from the movie *Risky Business*, "Sometimes you just gotta say 'What the fuck.'" And when his father demanded he go to Yale, though all he wanted to do was go to art school, he made his move, packed up his things, and headed south with hardly a backward glance. It helped to have a trust fund and a pretty awesome, albeit aging, Range Rover, but honestly, material things didn't matter much to Spence. Give him some blue sky, a sunny day, a handful of diving pelicans, and the perfect wave, and he was a happy man.

It took Ben all of about three minutes to show up, a bag of Tostitos and a jar of salsa in tow.

"I brought dinner." He shook the bag of chips.

"Careful—that's precious cargo in your hands. Don't want shattered chips." He opened a bottle of local IPA for his friend.

"Thought I'd see you at the beach today—where were you?" Ben took a swig of his beer then unscrewed the salsa lid from the jar. He dumped a bunch of chips on the small table between them as he sat down in the folding chair next to Spencer.

"Nice. A good clean surface to eat from."

Ben shrugged. "And that matters because?"

Spencer nodded. "Good point." He grabbed a chip and dipped it into the jar. "Yeah had a tragic event occur this afternoon." He hung his head, chin to chest.

Ben looked at him. "Huh. Don't see any blood. No

bruises. No stitches."

Spence shook his head. "Far worse than bodily harm, my friend. It's Petie." He frowned.

Ben lifted an eyebrow. "Petie? You break your fin?"

Spencer heaved a sigh. "I wish." He took a swig of his beer. "Some batshit crazy chick backed into my car and my board was on the back and she snapped it in half." He held a chip aloft between his fingers and broke it for emphasis.

Ben's brown eyes grew wide. "She killed Petie?"

"Trust me, I'd never lie about such a thing."

"What'd you do?"

He shrugged. "What was I gonna do? Not like I could punch a woman or anything. And all I wanted to do was cry but that wasn't happening."

"So, you just stood there?"

He nodded. "Pretty much. Crazy lady with the dinged-up car kept saying crazy things, then she wrote me a check to fix my board even though I can't fix it, and she drove away."

"A check?" Ben said, spinning his finger to his head to indicate that alone was nuts. "Is this like 1990 or something?"

"Right? Who writes a check anymore?" Spencer ran his fingers through his hair. "And on top of it all, I didn't get to go out on the water today, and it was so perfect, and I know the waves were amazing."

Ben pursed his lips. "I'd be lying if I didn't say they were the best they've been in weeks."

Spencer held up his hand. "Say no more. Bad enough day—no need to make it worse."

"Can I see Petie one last time? Or did you read him last rites and send him off to the fishes?"

"That's not a bad idea, give him a proper burial at sea.

Petie would like that. But right now, he's in the garage. I don't have the heart to look at him in that state." He took a long draw from his beer, finishing the bottle, then grabbed another.

"I don't blame you, man." Ben tipped the neck of his bottle to his friend's. "To Petie, dude. He was a helluva board."

The men sat in silence on the roof as the sun crested below the waves, scattering barbs of violet and peach and magenta as if Mother Nature had spilled bottles of tempera paint across the surface of the ocean.

"You gonna make another Petie?"

Spencer scrubbed his face then took another swig of his beer. "Man, I dunno." He grimaced. "I've got that board I was working on for my brother, but I feel like I'd be a douche to keep it for myself. And I don't have the time to make another one. I've been so busy with work." By day Spencer was a bicycle courier. "And by nighttime, I'm beat, man."

"I hear ya," Ben said. "But I think he'd understand. It's a board emergency. Besides, he's not gonna need it till next summer when he comes down here again."

"If he comes down here again."

"I thought he loved it here."

Spence shrugged. "He does. He came down here to manage the surf shop as an easy way to escape my control freak father, and he fell in love with the place as much as I did. But he's not as good at cutting the cord altogether as I was. He's still on track to finish that MBA program next year, so he might have to enter the real world. At least if the old man has a say in things."

"In other words, he isn't going to have much need for that board." Ben arched his eyebrow and grinned.

"Well, when you put it that way…" He furrowed his brow and looked at his friend. "Petie two?"

They clinked bottles. "Here's to the second time around."

"And to never encountering crazy blond women again."

"Hear, hear," Ben said with a laugh.

Chapter Five

AFTER her mom died, Georgie's mother's best friend, Margie Garfinkel, tried to fill the void created by her absence. Which meant regular outings to shop, eat, and gossip.

"Oh, Georgie, I can't believe you did that to that poor boy's surfboard," Margie said over margaritas and nachos.

Georgie blushed. "I know, right? Can you even stand that I destroyed this man's handiwork? I feel so awful about it, and I don't even have a way to reach out to him to apologize further."

Margie placed her hand on top of Georgie's. "Maybe that's just as well, sweetie. Strange men with rage issues can be a scary thing."

Georgie rolled her eyes. "Who said anything about rage issues?"

"Well, didn't he use the f-bomb on you?"

"Of course he did. Same as I would have if he'd ruined something that took me ages to make by hand. Not that I can imagine anything like that, but if there was." She was still entertaining the idea of making that quilt, but it seemed such a crackpot of a thing to do for someone she'd probably never see again.

"So, he wasn't enraged at you?"

Georgie scrunched her nose and thought about that for a minute. "Actually no, he wasn't at all enraged. He was surfer-dude chill. Surprising. I mean I'd be jumping up and down and screaming my head off. But his shoulders sank, his face fell. To be honest, he seemed more crestfallen, if anything." She thrust out her lower lip in a pout. "I feel awful about that."

"I'm so sorry, sweetie." Margie took a slug of her drink then smacked her lips. "Oooh-whee! They do make a good margarita here."

"Well the place is called Margarita Maggie's so they'd better. It's practically their calling card." She pursed her lips, deciding whether to clue Margie in on her idea.

"Something wrong, bug?" The term of endearment always made Georgie feel so loved.

"I was thinking of doing something as a sort of 'I'm sorry' gift for the guy. The only thing is I might not ever see him again, so it might be particularly weird to do something like that, you know?"

"Like what did you have in mind?"

"Remember when I made that quilt for Mom?"

She smiled, her eyes crinkling in that warm, loving way that melted Georgie's heart. "Of course! Your mama treasured that quilt—all that love and devotion you put into making it for her."

"I enjoyed making that. It was a good thing to do with my idle time too. Perfect for watching TV. So, I thought maybe I'd make an apology quilt. For a man, I'll probably never see. In which case, it'll be a penance quilt that I'll happily cherish." She giggled.

Margie nodded. "I, for one, think it's a lovely idea, dear. What man wouldn't appreciate that?"

Georgie figured it went without saying that Dan

wouldn't have appreciated it. Dan. What a jerk. How could she have been so stupid? She shook her head, trying to get rid of thoughts of that miserable excuse for a man.

"You okay?" Margie cocked her head.

"I'm fine. All good." She scooped up a chip with lots of cheese and ground beef on it. "I'm thinking about what a schmuck I was to have fallen for Danny Leonard."

"You weren't a schmuck."

"Okay, a fool."

"Not that, either." She patted her hand again. "You were a lonely young woman missing her beloved mama who fell for a man who turned out to be a coward. That was not at all about you, Georgie." Margie pulled her chin toward her with her pointer finger. "You know that, don't you?"

Georgie shrugged. You can't be left behind weeks away from a wedding and not take it personally. But she didn't want to get into the nuts and bolts of it right now, so she simply agreed with Margie. "Yeah, I know."

"And I bet if he were ever brave enough to come back here, he'd apologize profusely to you."

"If he ever came back here, I'd kick him in the balls and send him packing."

They both burst out laughing. "I would be right behind you, maybe with a strong left hook."

"Now that I'd love to see," Georgie said, pretending to throw a punch.

"But let's forget about Dan. He's history, and there's no reason to ruin a perfectly good couple of margaritas talking about him. Tell me what else makes you happy these days, Georgie."

She cast her gaze skyward, thinking for a minute, trying to come up with something. "I've been enjoying working with Harper Landry at her shop. She's sweet and funny, and she's even teaching me how to make jewelry." She held out her wrist, on which rested a simple silver band with a swirl in the center of it.

"Did you make that?"

Georgie nodded. "With my own hands. I guess another craft I can add to my crafty resume."

"You have a crafty resume?"

"Well, I guess informally. I tried to figure out if I had any interesting skills other than scrolling through Facebook too often." She sighed. "Ugh. Facebook. It's going to be the death of us all, isn't it?"

"I hear ya. I decided to go on a Facebook fast for the next month to see if I miss it."

"I bet you won't."

"I bet you're right." Margie winked at her. "You can join me. Instead of wasting time on the computer, why don't you get to work on that quilt?"

Georgie curled her lip. "You don't think it's weird to make it for him when I'll never see him again?"

"I think it's a delightfully optimistic thing to do. In fact, why don't we run to the quilt store after this and we'll find a pattern so you can get started on it? Maybe I'll look for something little to work on too. After all, we're going to have lots of time on our hands now that we're off of Facebook. Deal?" She extended her hand to meet Georgie's and they shook.

"We're going to be super uber productive. I can feel it in my bones."

"Well, who knew?" Georgia said as she thumbed through patterns and kits at the quilt store. "Apparently the good thing about a seaside quilt shop is that there are all sorts of ocean-themed patterns." She pointed to an already-finished quilt hanging on the wall. "I love that one. And there are so many different types of jellyfish! I would never have thought to make jellyfish quilts."

"I love them," Margie said, running her fingers along the Caribbean-blue background on which three-dimensional, multitextured fabric jellyfish were appliqued. "Which is funny—you know how much of a weenie I am in the ocean because I hate jellyfish. But in fabric form, they're downright elegant."

"Remember that time my mom and I literally dragged you into the water because you were so scared of them? We wanted to prove to you that you had nothing to be afraid of."

Margie shook her head. "Crazy for a grown woman to be afraid of something so insignificant, isn't it?"

"Totally understandable. We all have those things that scare us."

"Like for you, I'd venture to guess you're particularly scared about ever venturing into a new relationship."

Georgie pretended to thrust a dagger into her heart. "Guilty as charged. I can't foresee a time in which I'd want to be involved with another man. I think I'm going to take a vow of celibacy and join a nunnery. Although it seems as if that vow of celibacy has been in full force now for the past two years anyhow."

"Huh. Has it been that long already? Seems like plenty of time to heal a broken heart, no?" Margie glanced at

Georgie out of the corner of her eyes as she fondled fabrics.

"Even if my heart heals—and I'm not telling you it can or will—who's to say I ever want to risk injuring it again?"

Margie nodded. "As someone who has loved and lost and loved again, I hope you are willing to take that chance. Think of how much you might miss out on because you allowed fear to dominate your life. It's like those people who are so terrified of terrorism that they won't travel abroad—even though they have a far greater chance of being in a car accident in their own neighborhood. Fear is a terrible burden to carry around for your whole life, hon." She wrapped her arm around Georgie's shoulder.

"I know, I know." Georgie knew intellectually that her mother's friend was spot-on, but emotionally? There was the rub. It was far easier to, say, make a quilt for someone she'd never see again. That was the type of commitment her heart could handle. It was time to divert this conversation into something a little safer and more comfortable. "I wonder if a surfer would hate jellyfish? They wear wet suits to keep warm, but the suits probably protect them from those nasty tentacles too. So maybe they don't mind them?"

Margie held her young friend's cheeks between her hands and fixed her pale blue gaze on Georgie's. "It's okay. I'll let you change the subject on me. As long as somewhere in there," she paused, then rapped Georgie's head lightly with her knuckles, "you are registering what I'm saying. So that slowly but surely, you'll begin to realize how much you are denying yourself by allowing your fear to win out. Promise?"

"Yeah, yeah. I promise."

"And remember: those surfers? Even if they're scared

of what's lurking beneath the surface of the big, dark ocean, they keep returning to it, despite those fears. Jellyfish? Sharks? Inherent risks in pursuing their passion. Risks they're willing to take. And I trust that soon, you'll be willing to take your chances that there might be other sharks you could encounter, and understand that even if they take a bite out of your heart, you'll survive. And thrive."

Georgie knew Margie was speaking logic. And she hoped someday she could believe it. Until then, she would have to be perfectly happy quilting for men she'd never have to worry about again. It was much safer that way.

Chapter Six

SPENCER was hunkered down in his workshop, putting the finishing touches on what he'd started referring to as Pierre. It didn't seem right to call his new board Petie, but he also wanted to honor Petie in some way. So, he dubbed him the French counterpart, an homage of sorts. It sounded regal and classy. It had been six weeks since the day he'd started referring to as D-Day, for laughs. He figured if he didn't laugh about it, he'd probably cry, and he wasn't that kind of guy. Sure he was bummed about it. Big time. But he also wasn't one of those people who held on to his anger. Life was too short for that nonsense.

Instead he focused his free time on finishing his replacement board. He figured he'd slap a big red bow on it for Christmas and give it to Nate as a sort of IOU for his own surfboard. It would be awhile till he'd need one anyhow, so this way everyone would be happy. He'd finished fiberglassing the top, was about to install the fin box, and after that a final sanding and finish, and it was ready for its inaugural run.

He thought about how far he'd come in less than two months. He never imagined he'd have the board done for his brother in time; but now, not only was his board-to-be almost done, he'd gotten some work done on the replacement board for Nate as well. It helped that he'd been able to get out of work pretty regularly and, well, minus his favorite board, he hadn't been spending as much time in the water after work. Which meant he could devote some more time to crafting the boards. He started thinking about that blond chick who'd caused all the problems. He still felt bad for her—like he was a bit of a dick to the poor thing when she must've been hugely embarrassed after what she'd done.

In a way, he wished there was a chance for him to set the record straight, let her know it was okay. The other day, he'd pulled her check out from the kitchen drawer where he'd stuck it. He even gave a long, hard thought to calling her, but then thought better of it. He didn't have time in his life to deal with that type of thing. Plus after having been in her presence for a brief time, he feared she'd be one of those weirdo glommers he'd never be able to shake. He wasn't looking for another friend or a girlfriend, so it made the most sense to steer clear.

Spencer gave a tug on the zipper of his wet suit and braced himself for the brisk water. Not everyone was willing to go into the November-cold ocean to catch a wave, but he was hard-core, and besides, he had to test out Pierre. It was hard enough waiting for this day to arrive. He'd texted his buddy Noah Gunderson, a fellow surfer, to join him here.

"Haven't seen you around lately," Noah said as they paddled into deeper water. "I thought you'd found a new hobby."

"I swear it gives me PTSD every time I have to explain it, but some idiot woman driver nailed Petie in the parking lot a couple of ago."

"Nailed him?"

"Yeah, as in backed into him so hard he snapped in two."

"Ouch." Noah shook his hand as if it hurt.

"Tell me about it. I considered holding a funeral for him."

"That would've been good. I betcha a ton of us would have shown up." He laughed. "So, what's up with this board? It looks a lot like Petie."

"Yeah, well, it's like getting a new dog after your last one keels over. It's never going to be the same, but it'll ultimately be okay."

Noah laughed. "I guess I've never gotten so intimately attached to my surfboards before."

"It's weird, isn't it?" Spence said. "I dunno why I became so proprietary about the thing. I guess it's cause I grew up with everything handed to me on a silver platter. I never learned to value things much. When I learned how to make my own board, it gave me a sense of accomplishment I weirdly hadn't experienced before." He held up his finger as he started paddling hard to catch a wave. Noah was fast on his heels as they mounted their boards and rode the wave almost to the shore.

They plunked down on their boards to paddle out again. "I can respect that." Noah nodded. "And I'm sorry about Petie. But it looks like this board is going to do fine."

"It all comes out in the wash. Or so my nanny used to

say to me."

"Your nanny?"

Spence laughed, aiming his thumb at his chest. "Right? Hippie surfer dude me had a nanny."

Noah shook his head. "Goes to show you there's so much about a person you don't know. I'd have pegged you for being raised by wolves."

Spencer shook his head. "To be honest, I pretty much was. If it weren't for my nanny, I'd have probably grown up to be a predatory, greedy bastard like my father."

"Then here's to that nanny. She seems to have done you well." He tipped his head to him.

"Thanks, Noah. Yeah, my old man was all about worshipping at the altar of the almighty dollar." Spencer frowned. "He even took down his long-time partner in a surprise business coup because he was tired of sharing in the profits. When my parents split up, he tried hard to smear my mother to ensure she didn't see any of his cash. Lucky for her, she had a savvy lawyer, so she ended up fine, but not without the two of them duking it out in the cesspool for a good while. It was enough to send me packing. I wanted nothing to do with them or their lifestyle."

"Looks like you achieved that goal."

"Yeah, but it wasn't without its fallout." Spencer paddled fast to catch another wave, but it passed them both by too quickly. "I blew off college because my father was determined I was going to Yale the same way he did. No fucking way was I going to do that because he said I had to. I wanted to go to art school, but I never ended up doing it. Instead I loaded up my car and drove away from the family mansion in Connecticut. Never looked back." He shrugged.

"I felt bad because my little brother Nate was left

behind and had to deal with my asshole father. My mother was pretty upset, but I never saw her much anyhow—she was in the city by then, hobnobbing with the rich people in Manhattan. It wasn't my scene." He shook his head. "Oh, and I left my girlfriend behind as well. But that whole thing *was* her scene, so it wasn't going to last anyhow. She even sided with my father and he paid her to try to talk me out of leaving. At that point, I told her 'sayonara' and I bailed."

"And here I thought you were simply your average bicycle messenger. Who knew you had this sordid past?" They both laughed. "Let's see. You're not in touch with your folks. I know your brother was here working at the surf shop, so you two seem to be cool. And you never thought about reaching out to your old girlfriend to see if there was anything there?"

"I have no interest in dealing with girlfriends again for a while. When I decided to pull out of Connecticut, she took my dad's side. It ticked me off. She couldn't see how he was suffocating me so badly. Yet until then, I trusted that she was my ally." He readied himself for the next wave. "It left me bitter and not up for a relationship where I was going to be betrayed again. I'm good with Tinder, thanks."

Noah nodded. "Yeah, Tinder's a little limiting in small towns like Verity Beach, but it'll do in a pinch if you need to scratch that itch."

"As far as I'm concerned, that's all I need. Give me the perfect wave, my favorite board, and a hookup or two, and I'll never need to rely on another woman again."

Chapter Seven

GEORGIE was not a tea sandwich sort of gal. Give her a big cheesesteak, or a hoagie, and she was a happy camper. But some teensy triangle barely bigger than her thumb didn't count as food in her world. Who eats a cucumber sandwich, anyway? Or cream cheese on white bread? No wonder the things were so tiny—if you had to eat any more than that you'd cry "uncle."

Perhaps her beef wasn't so much with the silly tea sandwiches, or even the way some of the women here were literally sipping their pretentious tea with their pinky fingers sticking out—like they were the damned queen or something—but more with her Aunt Jeannie, who never met an occasion where she didn't try to one-up Georgie with her own daughter Marcy. And what better occasion to rub her daughter's superiority in Georgie's face than at Marcy's bridal shower.

"Georgie, are you sure you don't have any man you'd want to bring to Marcy's wedding? You're more than welcome to bring someone."

Patty, Georgie's mom, and her sister Jeannie were never much in the friends department. Jeannie had been super jealous when Patty married Georgie's dad, Bob. Evidently Jeannie had nurtured a burning crush on him in high school. It was one of those cliché things: Bob was the star quarterback, Jeannie, a cheerleader. As much as Jeannie tried to get his attention, he seemed to turn his attention instead toward the bookish younger sister, Patty. When it became abundantly clear she was not going to land her football hero, Jeannie's claws came out for Patty and their relationship suffered for it.

It became worse when they both had children, as Jeannie always felt the need to prop up her daughter against Georgie. Marcy's glossy black hair was so much prettier than Georgie's dishwater-colored waves. Marcy's eyes were a warm brown, while Georgie's were a cold blue. The gospel according to Jeannie. The irony was that Jeannie dodged a bullet with that one. Bob, it turned out, had a ferocious temper and Georgie's mother spent her marriage cowed in a state of anxiety and fear until eventually she mustered up the courage to leave him. But Jeannie could only blame her sister for being the root cause of Bob's anger; she was certain had she married him she'd have tamed him.

The only reason Georgie even bothered to maintain contact with her relatives at this point was that she had so few. She'd long ago cut ties with her father. His excessive drinking was bad enough but always led to outbursts and his blaming Georgie for her mother leaving. Even in death, she couldn't escape his blame. She'd tried to keep her father in her life, but a couple of years of therapy helped her realize she was better off without him in it. So that left her with Jeannie and Marcy, which was like being told you have a choice of eating four-day-old fish or overcooked, tough steak. She certainly didn't have a family smorgasbord from which to choose.

Sure it was frustrating that her Aunt Jeannie treated

her a bit like Cinderella. But she took solace in knowing that at least she wasn't her mother. And if she couldn't have her mama, at least she had Margie in her stead, the next best thing, and she knew that she was far better off than Marcy, who was stuck with a miserable mother desperately trying to live vicariously through her daughter. If left to her own devices, Marcy could be okay. But she'd been so browbeaten by her mother, that she obviously failed to come out from under her thumb.

"It's a shame you haven't been able to keep a man, Georgie," Jeannie said as she passed a plate of petit fours—another desperately failed attempt at dessert. Give her a fat chunk of chocolate cake, or maybe an oversized serving of apple pie, thanks. But a tiny square of some baked thing covered with plastic-tasting icing? Thanks, but no thanks. "Marcie was practically turning down suitors when James came to call."

Jesus, Georgie dreaded how badly her aunt could humiliate her at the actual wedding if she was already laying it on so thick here. To think she took a bath and fixed her hair and put on a nice dress only to come to this cheesy bridal shower tea party and be swiped at by a mean-spirited aunt. *Haven't been able to keep a man…* What a beyotch she was!

"I'm totally good, Aunt Jeannie," Georgie said, holding her hand up in protest. "I've got a few truly excellent vibrators. The great thing is you don't even need batteries anymore—charge it up when you plug in your cell phone, and you're good to go. Between that and all that free online porn, who needs a man anymore? They're a needless hassle and leave their dirty underwear and socks lying around anyway."

Her aunt's near-black eyes grew wide and her mouth

drew open in exclamation, causing her to drop the tea sandwich she'd started to shove into her mouth. The fallen, deconstructed sandwich with its cucumber bits scattered on the table beneath her aunt and made Georgie feel all warm and fuzzy inside.

Georgie looked around her aunt's living room at the seven bridesmaids who were trying hard not to crack up. She glanced at Marcy and mouthed, "I'm sorry" to her, and luckily Marcy waved her hand and mouthed back, "no worries." That left her fiancé's mother and grandmother who it seemed was quite hard of hearing and missed the comments altogether. She suspected the mother chose to unhear what Georgie had said. But her aunt, well, she looked as if she could easily have been working up a full head of steam that would soon blast from all orifices in her skull. Instead she threw a hard stink-eye at Georgie and continued on as if she'd not heard the offending statement.

"I think this calls for a toast, to our Marcy, who fended off a lot of Mr. Maybes before finding her Mr. Right." She held her champagne glass high as everyone agreed.

Georgie did her level best to not stick her finger down her throat and gag. *Mr. Maybes her ass.* Georgie was looking for *Mr. I Couldn't Give a Shit* at this point. And by that she meant she couldn't give one shit. Or two, for that matter. All this blather about marrying—she was so over it. There was no such thing as Mr. Right or Mr. Wrong. There were flawed men who would ultimately break your heart, maybe even when you least expected it. Like when you only have a few weeks before nuptials are exchanged and rings placed on fingers.

She didn't know how she was going to get through this wedding without getting stinking drunk and calling out her aunt for her obnoxious ways. She'd need to bring reinforcements, which meant her friend and boss Harper was going to have to be her plus one and her bodyguard. Otherwise, Lord only knew what she might regret doing.

Chapter Eight

GEORGIE drew her needle through the edge of the appliqued stingray as she took her final stitch on the ocean creatures quilt for her anonymous victim. After going on her Facebook-free diet she found she had an inordinate amount of free time, so she'd been working diligently on her quilt. Every idle moment she had she created the various blocks on which she'd hand-stitched an octopus, a crab, a jellyfish, a seahorse, a fish, a turtle, a stingray, a hammerhead shark, a swordfish, a sea otter, and even a mermaid. The last block featured a wooden surfboard. She hadn't gotten a good look at the guy's board, but this was a reasonable enough facsimile to get the point across. She planned to spend the afternoon stitching the blocks together; then she'd be ready to hand-quilt it together, which was a perfect project for the cold nights that had set in. And the ideal distraction to keep her from nonstop dreading the upcoming wedding.

She was taking a break to make a grilled cheese and heat up some tomato soup when Margie called.

"Hey sweetie," she said. "I know that wedding is looming large for you. Just wanted to call and see if you've found someone to take. I'm perfectly happy to go with you, but I know you don't particularly want to bring an old gal like me."

Georgie flipped her sandwich on the pan and gave the soup a stir. "You know I'd love to have you there, but I also would hate to subject you to Aunt Jeannie. I'll be fine. After my vibrator comments to her, I think she'll to steer clear of me anyhow."

Margie laughed. "I have to hand it to you, Georgie. That was a stroke of sheer genius to pull that one out. I wish I had thought of it myself."

"I'm not sure where my remark came from, but I'm glad I thought of it. I need to learn to be armed with zingers like that to shut her up more regularly." She put the sandwich on her plate and cut it in half diagonally, then poured the soup into a mug. "So, Harper's coming with me. She's kind of seeing this guy, but he never seems to be around, and I think there's some other ex-boyfriend she's trying to shake, so I figured it would be good for us both to have each other's backs a bit."

"If you're certain?"

Georgie dipped the corner of her sandwich into her soup and took a chomp. She rolled her eyes back. Nothing like a good grilled cheese on a cold night. "I'm so good. I'll let you know how it goes."

"Can't wait to hear. And remember, behave."

Georgie laughed. "Surely you don't think I would do something to embarrass myself."

"Not yourself, but with that aunt of yours, you never know what you'll do if she pushes your buttons."

"Okay, well, I'm going to push the off button here right now so I can eat my sandwich and get back to my quilt. Love you!"

As much as Georgie would love to stick it to old Aunt Jeannie, she wouldn't do that to her cousin. She'd have to save it for some other time.

Georgie decided it was best to drive so she could control when she arrived and when she left the big wedding bash. She figured she'd be there till the canapés were passed and then blow out of there, soul intact. And she was certain Harper would be glad to leave as soon as possible as well. Maybe they could go for a drink somewhere with a nice warm, cozy fireplace and could toast to their singlehood and lack of men in their lives. Although Harper had some guy lurking around. And maybe another one, for that matter. She wasn't letting on too much, but that was the best Georgie could discern, based on Harper's vague comments.

Georgie decided to go all-out and look her damnedest for this thing—she wasn't going to give her aunt a reason to fault her. So what that she might need to lose ten or fifteen pounds. To hell with that. She was perfectly happy the way she was.

She pulled on a silver silk dress with a flared sheer floral silver organza overlay. The high-waisted dress was scooped at the neck and landed midcalf. Once her dress was on, she finished her hair, lacing the blond strands into a French braid that helped to emphasize her beautiful icy blue eyes. She even finger-curled the tendrils that she couldn't catch into the braid.

She slid her feet into a pair of glittery silver pumps that

Margie had lent her. And Margie had expensive taste, so she didn't doubt they cost a small fortune. Taking a look at herself in the mirror, she grinned—she loved herself exactly as she was. If her aunt couldn't see that, well that was her problem.

After she picked up Harper, they drove to the wedding venue, a charming restored Victorian manor located on the beach. They climbed the wide porch steps and entered a cozy living room with a fire blazing in the fireplace. There, a woman led them through a large dining room, then outside to a deck with a clear plastic-covered, heated area set aside with rows of chairs. Hundreds of candles twinkled both inside and outside the tent.

Sometimes she especially hated that her aunt always made things perfect. And it made her particularly sad because her mother would have found something even more perfect for her, had she been alive still. Had she actually gotten married. Neither of which were realities, unfortunately. She looked over at Harper, who seemed particularly distracted by a handsome man who'd started talking to her as if he knew her. Georgie approached them to see if she needed help.

"Sorry. Didn't mean to be rude. Georgia, meet Noah."

Georgia glanced at Harper, surprised. "Noah as in *that* Noah?"

Noah had been Harper's serious boyfriend for ages but had abandoned her years earlier. Harper had mentioned running into him a couple of times and that she wanted to get him off her back.

"This is the Noah I might have mentioned before."

Georgia shook his hand as if she'd touched something hot. "Damn, girl, you failed to tell me that he looked like this. No wonder you were pissed at him leaving."

The corner of Noah's mouth curled up into a grin. He reached his hand out. "Georgia—delighted to meet you. How do you two beautiful women know each other?"

What a charming man! Georgie needed to get to the bottom of why Harper would want to get rid of him. He was adorable and so sweet.

"Please, call me Georgie. I'm Harper's right-hand woman in the shop."

"Oh? What shop is that?"

Georgia threw a side glance at her friend. "He doesn't even know about the shop?"

Harper frowned. "Um, no?"

"I'd love to hear more about this mystery shop."

Harper shook her head. "Stop mocking me. It's not a mystery. I simply didn't want to share my private business with you. I reserve that for people I trust."

Georgie licked the tip of her finger and tapped the air, making a sizzling sound. "The score: Harper, one. Noah, zero."

Noah—who apparently ran the place—ushered them to their seats. Georgie leaned over to her friend. "So, this is the guy you're trying to get rid of? Sheesh. I'd hate to see the guy you're hot on if this one isn't good enough for you."

Harper shook her head. "It's complicated. Trust me on that. I'll fill you in later." She put her finger to her lips. "The wedding is about to begin."

Which meant that poor Georgie now had to have her aunt's good fortune rubbed in her face once more. She couldn't wait for this day to end.

Chapter Nine

LIKE it or not, Georgie had to admit Marcy looked stunning. She was elegant in a classic ivory sheath that brought to mind Audrey Hepburn. The silk and lace gown hugged her slim body and made her look model thin. She couldn't wait to hear how Aunt Jeannie would compare her stronger, fuller physique to her svelte daughter's. Bring it. Maybe Georgie could be double-fisting doughnuts while she bore the brunt of her insults.

Marcy practically glided down the aisle, her besotted father fighting back tears, her mother beaming with the glow of victory.

But enough about her. Marcy looked overjoyed, her broad smile betraying any silly familial hostilities that might create a subtext to her big day. Her fiancé—James something or other—had broken out into a huge grin as soon as he saw his bride. The two of them clasped hands, and he gave her an adorable kiss even before the vows were exchanged. Georgie was happy for them. She had to remember not to conflate Marcy with her mom because Aunt Jeannie's behavior certainly wasn't her fault.

The sun was setting as they finished exchanging their vows. The late-day sun reflected off the water, and soon the pink glow warmed the view considerably. It's what

Georgie loved so much about living at the ocean. You could have a perfectly shitty day and take one look at that sunset over the cresting waves and all would be good with the world.

Nevertheless, she needed a drink. Stat. It was stressful being the ugly-duckling relative at your cousin's wedding. Even if you weren't truly an ugly duckling, and it was only that Cinderella's stepmom kept telling you that you were. Either way, it was time for a cocktail, and fast.

The friends made their way to the bar, but Noah intercepted them and offered to get them drinks. Georgie practically pleaded for a Tito's on the rocks. She tempered it with a splash of sparkling water and lime, even though ideally, in her heart of hearts, she wanted two fat fingers of vodka, straight up, to throw down her gullet and soften the blow of this event.

"So, you gonna fill me in on what's up with Noah? Or will I have to keep guessing?"

Harper rolled her eyes. "I can't get into it here. But Noah is a ghost from my past who insists on haunting me. And it's plucking my last nerve."

"Sure it's not tweaking your ovaries a little bit?" Georgie said with a wink. "I caught you stealing glances at him during the wedding. Maybe you two have some unfinished business you still need to resolve?"

"I honestly don't need that drama in my life. Everything is finally good for me, and I don't need a blast from the past to drop a load of cement on me right now."

Georgie shrugged. "Fair enough. In that case, here's to letting go of the losers, then." They clinked glasses and laughed as they threw back their drinks perhaps faster than they should have.

Noah approached again. "Look who I found all alone

and needing company," he said, his hand on a man's shoulder. "Harper, I think you might recall meeting Spencer at the bar recently, right?"

Harper reached out to shake his hand. "Great to see you again. And this is my date for this evening, Georgie Childress."

Georgie looked up only to realize it was him! The surfboard dude. She was sure of it. Only tonight, he had his longish sandy-blond hair pulled back in a bun. Which normally wasn't her thing, but damn, it looked hot. Instead of that wet suit, he wore a surprisingly conservative-looking charcoal pinstripe suit, with a crisp medium-blue shirt and coordinating gray flannel tie. She felt that tingle in her belly that had become so unfamiliar to her, but now she recognized it as what it was: lust. Oh God. She was hot for the guy whose surfboard she destroyed.

Spencer, not even looking up, reached for Georgie's hand and pulled it toward his mouth. "Enchanté," he said, as he kissed the top of her hand.

"Uhhh, yeah," Georgie said squinting her eyes. "You seriously don't remember me?"

He lifted a brow, then winced as he started to snap his fingers. "Oh, man. You." He pointed his finger at her. "You're the surfboard-killer chick."

Harper looked from her friend to Spencer and back again. "Should I ask?"

Georgie shook her head. "Trust me, it's so not worth knowing."

She had been too embarrassed about her accident to share it with anyone other than Margie, who she knew wouldn't judge her.

Harper shrugged. "Okey dokey, then." She mouthed to her friend, *You'd better fill me in on that later.*

The wedding director announced they were about to present the wedding party, which meant they all had to take their seats immediately. Hopefully that meant she could avoid the surfer dude, while at some point getting his contact information so that she could maybe anonymously send him his quilt or something. Though damn, she'd grown to love that quilt. Shame she had to give it up. But she did, no two ways about it.

She was about to walk to the farthest table in the room when Noah led them to one too close to the wedding party than she'd have preferred, and then he proceeded to seat surfer dude—Spencer, was it?—smack-dab to her left. Which meant it was going to be an awkward mealtime, for sure.

Chapter Ten

WELL, damn. What a strange coincidence. Just as he finishes his board, he runs into the perpetrator. Go figure! He mentally double-checked that it wasn't mounted on the back of his car outside. Didn't want her to do a command-performance with this one. His heart couldn't take it.

He took a long, slow look at her. Before, all he'd noticed was her tears. How could he have gotten past that in the craziness of that episode? Tears and snot in large quantities. But looking at her now, he could see she cleaned up pretty well. She was taller than he recalled, with broad shoulders, perhaps like a swimmer or a rower. She looked like she could kick your ass if need be, but more than likely she seemed to be one of those people who would give you a big bear hug and congratulate you on a job well-done. Her gorgeous sea-blue eyes were fringed with long, full lashes. In fact, she was strikingly beautiful.

Which was good news, since he was stuck distracting her for the rest of the evening so that Noah could have his way with Harper, as per Noah's request earlier in the evening.

As a waitress served their entrees, Spencer turned to Georgie. "So, uh, Georgie. You do any more harm with that car of yours lately?"

She blushed, which he found awfully endearing. "Um, well, gosh, it's not like I do that sort of thing every day!" She frowned. "Do you really think I do?"

He held up his hands. "I was only making a joke. I have no idea about your driving skills. Although I did notice your car was a little banged up."

"Yeah, well, I've had it a long time." She eyed him and bit her lip. "I hope you accept my apologies for that. I felt super bad about it. But that reminds me, were you able to fix it?"

He arched his brow. "Did ya get a look at the thing? It was snapped in two."

"So, you had to toss it?"

He shrugged. "Didn't have the heart to toss it altogether. It's in my garage, awaiting a brainstorm about what to do with it."

Georgie pursed her lips. "What if you turned it into a couple of little coffee tables?" She rested her hand on her chin as she thought it out. "Like could you do something to finish off the ends and then do that? You could make matching end tables, and then you'd have your board with you all the time. Maybe you could even start selling your tables—call it Broken Board Designs."

He smiled. "That's not a half bad idea. I'll have to give that some more thought."

After dinner Harper excused herself to go the restroom, leaving Georgie and Spencer on their own.

"You got somewhere to go?" Spence asked after Georgia looked at her watch for the tenth time.

She looked up. "Huh? Oh, no. Sorry. I was wondering where Harper was. She and I had a pact that we weren't going to stick around here and once dinner ended was my cue to get the hell out of Dodge."

"You don't like weddings or something?"

She shrugged. "It's not that I don't like weddings. Even though I'm not exactly keen on them, if I were to be honest with you. But it's this wedding in particular."

"Because?" He turned his chair, so he was facing her.

"I have my reasons."

"What's got you so unhappy about this one?" He pointed at Marcy and James. "The bride is beautiful and the groom looks happy. Seems like a nice couple of families getting together to celebrate. What could possibly be so wrong about it?"

Georgie heaved a heavy sigh. "The bride's my cousin. And I'm fine with her. I mean fine enough. It's only that her mother is such a bitch to me. She's like Cinderella's stepmother." She frowned. "It doesn't help matters that I don't have my own mother anymore, so instead all I have left is her to browbeat me and always show me up with her perfect daughter."

Spencer's eyes opened wide. "Wow. That's a lot to

digest. I'm sorry."

She shrugged. "Yeah, well, we all have our crosses to bear. Except now I'm ready to shrug that old cross off my shoulders and get the hell out of the wedding, but my date has disappeared."

"This is where I make a confession." Spencer glanced from side to side, as if he was looking to be sure no one heard him.

"You kidnapped Harper? Locked her in a closet? Cast a spell on her?" She laughed. "Sorry, guess I got carried away with the evil stepmother theme there."

"As a matter of fact, while it was pure coincidence that I ended up at this wedding—I work with James—I was enlisted by Noah to be his wingman of sorts."

"Wingman?"

"Yeah, I'm supposed to help Noah get Harper alone. Which I guess also means I'm supposed to entertain you so that you aren't trying to find Harper to leave."

Georgie squinted at him. "Well of all the shitty things—"

He held up his hands in protest. "It wasn't meant to be a jerky thing. Noah believes he and Harper have things to resolve, and since she seemed to be avoiding him, he thought this would be an ideal time for him to get her alone."

"What if she doesn't want to be alone? Though I did catch her with that horndog look in her eyes every time she glanced his way."

Spencer laughed. "Telltale signs."

"So, this means Harper's not coming back anytime soon?"

"I'm afraid not. Looks like it's you and me, kid."

"It's fine. I'm perfectly capable of leaving her on my

own. You don't need to be my babysitter."

"I'm not being your babysitter. I've enjoyed talking with you. Especially when you're not destroying my cherished possessions."

She smirked at him. "Ha-ha. I feel badly enough about that—you don't need to rub it in. Well." She yawned and stretched her arms. "Here's hoping Harper and that ex of hers have found a king bedroom in this huge bed and breakfast where they can iron out their differences. If that's what they call it nowadays."

"Let me at least escort you home."

She held her hands up. "Hey, no need for formalities on my part. If you feel like you have to do that to fulfill your duties to your friend, be my guest. But I'm perfectly fine on my own."

Only for some reason, Spencer hated the idea of letting her leave alone, especially under the circumstances. No. He was going to make certain she got home safely and preferably tear-free this time.

Chapter Eleven

GEORGIE found it weird that this guy was following her home as though he were her bodyguard. She certainly didn't need that kind of treatment. She was strong and intelligent and perfectly capable of taking care of herself. She never got rides home from anywhere else after dark. Why would she need that now?

But then again, the guy was kind of cute and it was slightly chivalrous, even though his ulterior motive was so that Noah could get into Harper's pants. She shook her head. *Men—the games they play.*

She pulled up in front of her townhouse, which sat at the end of a quiet beach road. After opening the garage door, she pulled her car inside. Purse in hand, she walked toward Spencer, who was parked in the driveway, his car still running.

"So, I guess here's where we shake hands and say it's been nice meeting under other circumstances," she said, giving him a nod.

But he turned off the car, pulled his key from the ignition, and stepped out of the car.

"The night is still young," he said. "I thought you'd invite me in for a drink."

She knit her brow. That was mighty presumptuous of

him. But she did kill his board. And she could give him the quilt. Except it wasn't done yet, so no, she wanted to hold off on that. Eh, what was the harm in inviting him in for a short while? Noah knew him; it wasn't like he was some creepy stalker.

"Fine, if you insist—but one drink. I'd like to get to bed on the early side tonight."

"But it's a Saturday night. Do you work tomorrow?"

"No, but I'd like to go to bed, if that's all right by you."

The truth was, there was something about him that kept stirring things up inside her, and she was ready to call it a night and retire to bed with one of those vibrators she'd freaked out her aunt with. Time to cut to the chase and call it a night.

She unlocked the front door and let him in. They walked up a flight of steps into an open living room that overlooked the ocean.

"Nice place," he said. "Greatest view on earth."

"Well, there are probably nicer views—"

"I mean the ocean. It's gorgeous. Anytime anyone has an ocean view, it's the best view going. I could watch it all day long. It's like meditation for me."

She shook her head. "I so agree. It calms me. Well, except when I drive into people's surfboards." She laughed.

"Yeah, well, accidents happen."

"Will you forgive me?"

He nodded. "If you give me that drink you promised me."

She cocked an eyebrow. "I promised you a drink?"

"Yeah, somewhere between my groveling and my groveling."

She smiled. At least he acknowledged it. She motioned

to the sofa. "Give me your coat and pull up a seat."

She went to the kitchen and poured two tumblers of bourbon, then handed him his glass as she sat down next to him.

"So," she said, taking off her shoes and resting her feet on the coffee table. Because what was she going to say? It was all a bit awkward, him being here simply to keep Harper with Noah. It was as though she were being babysat.

"So, yourself." He sipped his drink. "Tell me: what makes Georgie tick?"

She sat with that for a minute. *Huh?* No one had asked anything like that before.

"Ummm… I have no freaking idea what makes me tick." She screwed up her face, unhappy with that lame answer.

"Nothing? You can't think of a single thing?" he asked. "Let me help prompt you. Plastic or paper? Dog or cat? Whiskey or wine?" He held up his drink. "I suppose you already answered that one. How about boxers or briefs?"

"Okay, okay. Let's see. Neither with the bags. I use my own bags when I go to the grocery store."

"Of course you do."

"What's that supposed to mean?"

He shrugged, taking a sip of his drink. "Nothing. You seem like the type of person who would do that. You drive a beat-up old Volvo. That means you carry your own grocery bags."

"That sounds like an insult, but I'm not going to take it that way. What do you use?"

"Neither. I hardly ever go to the store. If I do, it's a case of beer or one of those lifetime supply packages of toilet paper or paper towels, and they don't fit in a bag. If it's a couple of other things, I'll toss them in the car."

Georgie shook her head. "Men."

"What's that supposed to mean?"

"Nothing. Only that men are so damn simplistic. It's like you're boiled down to the basics. Kind of like babies: eat, drink, sleep, go to the bathroom. And not in that particular order."

He belted out a laugh. "Now that is hilarious. I don't think I've ever been compared to a baby before."

"Well, consider yourself compared."

He nodded. "Fair enough. You're entitled to your opinion. But remember, you're the one who blubbered over my broken board. Isn't it babies who bawl?"

She frowned. "No comment. Next question."

"Okay, then. Dog or cat?"

"Why must I choose? Can't I have one of each?"

"I'm not making you get one. I'm asking which you'd prefer."

"Well, I prefer both. And if you can throw in a bunny, I'd appreciate it."

He pulled out a pretend pen from behind his ear and a pretend notepad from his pocket. "Don't forget the bunny. Check. So then next on the list: boxers or briefs."

"Don't even get me started on that one," she said.

"Sorry, I already have. Continue."

"Fine. But it's gonna be a rant."

"Rant away."

"All right, so Danny insisted on tighty-whities. I hated them so much. They reminded me of my dad, who would get drunk and storm around the house in his saggy-assed tight whites, which were always more gray, screaming and hollering and pitching a fit. I can't disassociate briefs from that, so I unequivocally detest them. I tried to get Danny to change them. I bought him some of those sexy Italian bikinis, but he said they were gay. And that of course pissed me off because a) what does that even mean and b) there is nothing wrong with someone who is gay. And c), if they were gay, or if they meant you were gay, then at least gay men wore better underwear than he did." She stopped for a breath but was just getting started.

"I tried boxers with him. He said things hung too loose. What the hell? I mean half of America wears them, don't they? And they're all suffering from loose bits? Really? I liked the boxer-brief option, especially if they were in black, because they didn't evoke those awful memories of my jerk dad. They're sexy, and it would solve that looseness issue. But Danny would never change a thing about the way he wanted his life to be."

Spencer had thrust his bottom lip out into a frown. "Danny?"

She shrieked a little, taking a large sip of her drink to accompany the sound. "Danny. The man I thought I wanted to marry. That is until he backed out of the wedding precisely two weeks and six days before it was scheduled. *That* Danny."

Spencer whistled. "This guy Danny did that to you? What a complete douchebag."

She nodded aggressively. "Tell me about it. Do you know how much money it costs to pay for a canceled wedding?"

"You should've made him pay for it."

"Yeah well, good luck with that because along with his backing out, he up and disappeared. Gone like that." She snapped her fingers.

"On the one hand, I'm truly sorry," he said, reaching

out his hand to pat her on the shoulder. Except he missed and instead swiped her breast. "Sorry, didn't mean to do that."

"Apology accepted."

"But on the other hand," he continued, "I'm glad you didn't get stuck with him because the type of man who would do that is not the type of man you want to be stuck with for all eternity, you know?"

"Oooh, yeah. I do know that. Ultimately it was a blessing disguised as a flaming pile of dog poop that some prankster left on my doorstep to stomp out while in a pair of expensive stilettos."

"Yeah," he said, looking confused. "That. I suppose."

"My point is, yes, it was a gift, but a pretty shitty bit of packaging."

"So how long ago was it that Danny the Douche pulled the runner?"

"It's been almost two years," she said. "Two whole years since I—" She froze.

"Since you?"

"Nothing. Nothing. Let's say since I dated."

His eyes grew wide. "You haven't been on a date in two years?"

She stood and went back to the kitchen, bringing the bourbon bottle back with her. She refilled both glasses. "Nope. And that's fine by me."

"You know I was thinking, this is almost like Tinder, only without the sex."

"Tinder?"

"Yeah you know, the hookup app?"

"You use that thing?"

"Doesn't everyone?"

"Uh, no." She shook her head vehemently.

"Why not?"

"Because that seems to be like a huge disease factory waiting to happen." She stuck out her tongue. "Plus, ick. Thanks, no thanks. I'll settle for my vibrator."

Georgie no sooner got the words out than she blanched. *Did she honestly say that?*

"Oh my God. You didn't say that, did you?" Spencer closed his eyes and shook his head, no doubt trying to erase the mental image.

Georgie sensed the red of embarrassment sprinting up her neck and across her face. "Yep. Good ole Georgie 'No Filter' Childress, at your service." She heaved a sigh. "Bad enough that I already unloaded that one on my mean aunt."

"You told your aunt about your vibrator?"

She shrugged. "Well, it was more like telling her I didn't need the man she kept gloating that I couldn't get and keep, because, well, between my vibrator and online porn, who needs a man anymore?"

Spencer spat out his bourbon, then tried to wipe it off Georgie's nice white sofa using his jacket, with little success.

"Don't' worry about that. It's seen way worse." She waved her hand.

He tried to imagine what worse it might have seen.

"Get your head out of the gutter. Not *that* kind of worse."

"What do you mean?"

"Please. I know what you were thinking. You're a guy, after all."

He held his hands up in surrender. "Okay, so maybe I did think that. But I am a guy, after all. Besides, let's think this through to the logical conclusion. First off, you haven't even dated a guy in two years." He lifted his hand, counting off with his fingers. "Second, you haven't had sex with a guy in two years. And I'm betting that hardly even counts because it was with Douchebag Dan, who couldn't be bothered to change up his underwear for you, so I'm betting sex was perfunctory at best."

Georgie buried her face in her hands. "I cannot believe I am talking to a near stranger about the sex I'm not having and how bad the sex I once had was."

"We're not total strangers," he said. "After all, you did kill my surfboard. So, we're at least acquaintances, on an as-needed apology basis."

"There is that." Georgie started to think about this. She didn't know him yet made him a quilt. Was that so much different from throwing caution to the wind and having a one-night stand with the guy? Wasn't he paving the way to that suggestion?

People have one-nighters all the time, don't they? Sometimes you simply need to scratch an itch. She looked at him, admiring how handsome he was in what remained of his suit. He'd removed his suit jacket and had loosened his tie, unbuttoned the top button. His sleeves were rolled up a little bit so she could see that stretch of forearm that looked so sexy on a man. She remembered him with his wet suit slung low on his hips. That broad chest, the smattering of gold chest hair. The perfect amount to play with but not so much that he was a hairy beast.

Could she simply say "fuck it" and sleep with him? Besides, he knew Noah and Noah had known Harper for much of their lives, and she knew Harper, so he was practically family.

"I'm only saying, maybe your sofa needs to see *that.* And while I'll gladly offer up my services, it certainly doesn't need to be me. But seriously, Georgie. Two years?

You sure that thing"—he pointed toward her crotch— "hasn't petrified in that time period? You might want to double-check. Or I'll be happy to check for you." He gave her a broad grin.

Chapter Twelve

SPENCER could not believe he was having this conversation with the nutty chick who killed his board. Who ended up being sweet and cute and surprisingly delightful company. At first he'd viewed her as a woman he needed to distract to help Noah out, but now he was grateful Noah set him up to do that. He hadn't had such interesting conversations with a woman since, well, ever. Plus she had a great rack. And he'd love to show her that Danny the Dickhead was probably the most lackluster lover she'd ever encountered. Poor thing probably thought that was all sex amounted to. But with a selfish prick like that, he was pretty certain it was all about him, and she deserved more.

"So, this Tinder thing," she said, scooting closer to him on the sofa. "Do you just, like, find someone on there and do it?"

He grinned. "I mean usually I'll meet up with someone at a bar, have a drink or two, see if we're compatible. It's not like we're meeting in a parking lot and banging in the back seat."

"And do you always have sex?"

He shrugged. "Not always."

"Do you have a lot of one-night stands?"

"No more than the average guy, I guess."

Georgie slid her hand on top of Spencer's, which had been resting on his thigh. He groaned. Her hand was mere inches away from his dick, and there was no way he was going to stop that thing from acting of its own accord with such proximity. It swelled in his pants.

"I was thinking," she said, turning toward him, so their faces were inches away from each other. "Maybe it's time for me to end that dry spell. After all, a vibrator's never gonna be the same as a warm, hard man."

Spencer gulped. "Fuck, Georgie. Please don't start something you aren't gonna follow through on."

"Oh, I aim to follow through on it," she said, leaning forward, so their mouths were but an inch apart. "Trust me, I keep my word." With that, she settled her lips on his and he let out a rumbling groan as he pulled her toward him, lifting her leg over his and straddling her atop his body, so her crotch was pressed up against his burgeoning erection.

"Right there, Georgie. Right there." Spencer squeezed his hands against her ass to encourage her to move against him. He dragged his tongue along her lips, coaxing them open, and when she let him in, his tongue sought hers, stroking and licking and tangling with hers, exploring her mouth as they sought to learn the other's likes and dislikes.

Georgie's hands slid down to his collar where she unknotted his tie the rest of the way and threw it to the ground. Then she got busy unfastening the buttons of his dress shirt, making quick work of that, only to find a white tee beneath it, which she promptly lifted up and over his head.

Spencer couldn't believe his good fortune to have stumbled into this so unexpectedly. Here he thought Noah was kidding when he suggested that maybe Georgie would be his prize for the night, and sure enough, it looked like he was right about that. He glanced up at her, her lips red and wet from kissing, her hair already poking out from her French braids. Her eyes were wild with want. This was a woman who clearly needed a good fucking after a long, dry spell. And who was he to refuse a woman in need?

He reached behind her and tugged on her zipper, quickly sliding it to the base of her hips. He slipped the dress off her shoulders, leaving him in awe as her gorgeous breasts fell from the fabric that contained them. He couldn't decide fast enough where he wanted his hands, his mouth, his tongue. He pressed her farther against his cock with one hand and pressed against her back, encouraging her to lower her breasts to his mouth. Finally he was able to reach out and secure his lips around an areola, sucking and pulling with his hot mouth till he her nipple tightened against his tongue.

Quickly he moved to the other breast, licking and nibbling her nipple before taking it in his mouth. Georgie let out a moan that drove him mad. She was busily stroking her center against his hardness, but all that fabric from the dress was getting in the way. He wanted flesh on flesh, so he grabbed the hem of her dress and quickly lifted it over her head, tossing it aside. Finally, he could get a good long look at her with nothing hiding her but a skimpy pair of lacy panties. And he liked what he saw. A lot.

"You." She pointed at him. "Pants. Now." She grasped for his belt, unfastening it quickly, then the button, then the zipper, and she lifted herself up on her knees while she tugged his pants off. She gasped when she realized what was missing. "Commando?" she said. "You didn't give me that as one of my options."

"Sorry," he said, his tongue reaching to lick her lips as she pressed herself closer to his body. "Haven't done laundry in a while."

She laughed. "Like I said… Men."

"I'll show you a man," he said, reaching around and flipping her, so that she was on her back, spread against the cushions of the sofa. He dragged his tongue around her ear, twirling it as he followed the circles closer and closer to her ear. Licking along her jawline, he traced his tongue down her throat, his body pressed to hers, chest to chest, as he started to slide down hers, pausing again at those gorgeous tits. He pressed them together and licked one nipple and then the other like a kid in a candy store who can't choose between two lollipops.

He bit gently on a nipple and she moaned loudly. "Oh, you like that, do you?" he said.

"More," was all she could say. After bathing her breasts and nipples with his tongue for several minutes he moved farther down her body, playing at her belly button before trailing his tongue down to the edge of her panties.

He looked up at Georgie, who was watching him intently. "May I?" he asked.

"Hurry the hell up already," she said as she pressed her hand against his head, indicating with no uncertainty where she wanted his mouth to go. With his hands on her hips, he shimmied her panties off quickly and spread her legs so he could get to work.

Nothing made Spencer happier than pleasing a woman, and he never met a woman who didn't take great joy in his gift of creatively using his mouth to bring her to orgasm.

He stared for a moment at her wet slit before dragging his tongue in a long, slow swipe from her center to her clit.

Georgie shuddered as he took another pass with his tongue, then another, then inserted a finger inside of her. He circled her clit with his tongue before taking it into his mouth and sucking gently on it as he moved his finger in and out of her wet pussy.

Georgie pumped her hips, her breath coming fast and clipped. He spread her legs wider and pressed deeper with his mouth, burying his tongue inside of her while his nose stroked against her clit. Georgie's hips began to shake and tremble as she pressed his head into her pussy harder, riding his mouth as she climaxed, her body tensing and thrusting hard against him as he lapped up her juices flooding on his tongue.

No doubt about it, Georgie Childress was officially over her dry spell.

Chapter Thirteen

THE last time a man had his mouth on Georgie's pussy was back in college. And suddenly she couldn't for the life of her understand how she'd expected to go her whole life without a guy doing that to her again. Had she been stuck with Danny for the rest of her life, damn, she would have missed out… because that was something Danny refused to do. No way, no how.

He sure did her a huge favor by cutting bait and running. The only problem was she would now have to find someone else to do this on a semiregular basis. Despite how reliable her pocket rocket was, it could never achieve that level of nirvana. Nothing like a warm tongue to make everything okay. And if she was going to have even the slightest reservation about a shameless one-night stand, her experience with Spencer erased any such thoughts. His talented mouth alone was worth the price of admission.

Spencer reached for his pants, which were draped over the edge of the sofa. He quickly grabbed his wallet and pulled out a condom. Damn, for her, being prepared meant always carrying a Tide To Go stick in her purse. But for guys, well, they always had that emergency condom at the ready. Just went to show her how her sex life had declined—nowadays she only concerned herself with being ready to manage unexpected food stains.

He tore the wrapper with his teeth and quickly sheathed himself with the rubber, deftly rolling it onto his impressive cock as he slid up her body until his dick rested against her still-slick pussy lips. When he gave her a look that was plainly asking for permission, she answered by pulling his body toward her, pressing his glorious, tight surfer's ass with her hands. He dipped his hips slightly until the head of his cock spread the entrance to her body and ever so slowly, he pressed into her wetness as they both groaned loudly.

Once he'd seated his cock all the way in, he held still, pelvis to pelvis, and Georgie relished the feel of their sweaty bodies pressed together, the beat of his heart against her breasts. Soon Spencer slowly pulled out, then thrust more quickly, picking up the pace of his strokes. Georgie didn't want to let him slip out, so she wrapped her legs around his hips, bucking her own, meeting him thrust for thrust. He dipped his head down to one breast and caught the nipple in his mouth and sucked hard. Georgie moaned, then reached down between them and rubbed herself, desperate to climb back up to where she was moments ago when his mouth was on her.

Spencer's teeth clamped on her nipple, and Georgie felt it deep in her pelvis, kicking sensations into overdrive as a wave of spasms overtook her. Spencer drove his swollen cock deep into her once, twice, a third time before holding himself against her as her pussy contracted and the wave of an orgasm surged through her body and stars sparkled behind her closed eyelids.

They held tight to each other for several minutes as they rode out those last glimmering moments of climax. Georgie was worried she'd be hit with a bad case of buyer's remorse, but instead, she felt nothing but a warm, glowing pleasure.

Spencer tucked her head under his chin. "Damn," he said, and she could sense the warm rumbling of his voice against her ear. "I can say beyond a shadow of a doubt, that thing is not petrified."

They burst out laughing before drifting off to an unexpected sleep on her living room sofa.

Spencer woke again sometime around five in the morning. They'd both drifted off to sleep, only to wake up and make love again two more times before finally falling into a deep sleep. At some point during all that, they'd made it back to her bedroom, where he was comfortably nestled beneath a fluffy, feathered duvet. But now was the time he knew he needed to slip out. As much fun as they'd had, he was not one to stick around till daylight. That would imply there was something more to be expected of him, and there wasn't. He quickly slipped out from beneath the covers and tiptoed backward out the bedroom door and down the hall to the living room. He slipped on his pants, shoes, and shirt and gathered up the rest of his belongings before quietly leaving, taking care to be sure he locked the door handle on his way out.

Georgie thought she'd died and gone to heaven when Spencer woke her somewhere around two in the morning with his hard-on pressed against her back. They barely spoke a word as he turned her on her stomach and mounted her from behind, lifting her hips slightly with his hands and spreading her legs with his before sliding his cock into her warmth. There was something so intimate and arousing about being taken like that. Seconds later, he slipped his hand around and pressed his fingers into her slick center, her body pulsating until she came around his cock, with him quickly following.

Georgie had drifted off to sleep after the last time, thinking that perhaps in the morning she'd show him the quilt she'd been making, unbeknownst to him. She'd made a joke about it, how she hadn't known if she'd ever see him again and now here they were, suddenly on much more intimate terms than she could have ever imagined.

So, her disappointment was palpable when she woke to find him gone, no note, no nothing. Hardly a trace of him having been there. Were it not for the used condoms in her trash can, she might have believed she'd imagined the whole thing.

And curse her for having thought it was anything more than it was: a one-night stand. But it rankled her; how could anyone be so physically and emotionally close to someone, practically attached, and then up and walk away as if you'd simply shaken hands after a business meeting?

She closed her eyes and thought about how it felt with his tongue stroking along her wet center, and she shuddered as she remembered the pleasure he gave her. Or when she was on top, straddling him, while he suckled her breasts as she gyrated her hips and lifted and pressed down again and again on his hard cock till finally they both came hard, their bodies quivering with pleasure.

Spencer was right: she'd never had sex like that with Danny. With Danny, it was one and done, you're in, you're out. Wham-bam-thank-you-ma'am. He didn't try to please her; he simply wanted to get off himself.

So maybe it was a one-off with Spencer, and they'd never get naked again. But at least now Georgie knew there was something more out there, something better than her pocket rocket, and something way, way better than that loser Danny Leonard.

Chapter Fourteen

GEORGIE moped around the house all Sunday. It was raining out, one of those cold, late-November rains that chilled you to your bones. She made a fire in the fireplace and wished she had a cat. Or a dog. She made a mental note to maybe go to the animal rescue league and find one of each. She was tired of being alone and she finally wanted some company. If she couldn't find it in the human variety, then she'd happily settle for the canine or feline kind.

She forgot to set her alarm so ended up showing up late to work Monday morning. By the time she arrived, Harper was already into her second cup of coffee. She could tell because it took that many for Harper to look alert, like most people look as soon as they shower in the morning. Her friend was a slow riser.

"Well, good morning, glory," Harper said, offering up the cup of coffee she'd poured for Georgie, who took it with gratitude.

"Morning, yourself," Georgie said. "In case you were wondering, I'm all ears about where you got off to Saturday night."

Harper lifted an eyebrow. "Speaking of getting off... Likewise. I'm all ears about where you yourself got off on Saturday night, my pretty." She winked at her.

Crap. Did Spencer announce to everyone in Verity Beach that he banged Georgie after the wedding? It was bad enough she'd had to do a veritable walk of shame (granted, it was in her own bedroom, but still, the guilt was equally as fierce), but if he announced it to everyone at, say, brunch, on Sunday, ugh, well, that would suck.

Georgie bit her lip. "Uh, you first." She pointed at her friend.

"Okay, but you're not going to get away without confessing as soon as I spill my guts."

"Spill away."

"So, I went up to the bathroom and when I was coming out, Noah found me and pulled me into this big room where they store the linens. The next thing I knew, we were on the ground and our clothes were off and oh, Georgie, it was such a bad idea. I know I already said this, and Noah broke my heart something fierce, but every time we're together it's just right, you know?"

Georgie kind of knew. For the fleeting three or so times she and Spencer had made love, something about that felt so precisely perfect, it was almost painful to know it wasn't going to happen again.

"And then I came downstairs to find you and you were nowhere in sight. Before I knew it, Noah was driving me home. He has a way of persuading me, so he came inside and then we spent the rest of the weekend talking and making love and talking some more and then more sex and here we are!"

"To think I believed that warm glow about you had something to do with your second cup of coffee."

Harper smiled. "Trust me, this was way better than coffee." She turned to face Georgie, who was seated on the stool next to her at the display counter. "Now your turn.

'Fess up."

Georgie squinted. "What if there's nothing to confess?"

Harper cocked her head in disbelief. "I know you enough to tell a bluff when I see one. Spill."

"All right, all right. So yeah, we, um—"

"Hold it right there. Before you get to the 'um,' what was that surfboard killer thingy he said to you?"

Georgie rolled her eyes. "Ugh. I forgot he mentioned that. It's a long story, but basically a couple of months ago, I backed into his car where his board was mounted and I broke it. He said I killed his board. Which I did do. Though it wasn't on purpose. And I felt bad about it. I wrote him a check. Which, come to think of it, he never cashed, either." She sighed. "But see, he made it all by himself. It was a gorgeous board, best I could tell. But I killed it. I never thought I'd see him again. Except I wanted to somehow make an apology gift. So, I've been working on a quilt for him."

"Georgie, that is so sweet," Harper said. "You were making him a gift?"

She pursed her lips. "Kind of. In case I ever saw him again. But that didn't seem too likely. But just in case. And then there he was at the wedding. It was so weird."

"So, did you give it to him?"

Georgie started drumming her fingertips on the glass of the display case.

"Did something happen to it?"

"Can we change the subject?" She knew it was a stupid question, but she had to ask.

"No, we cannot change the subject. What happened? To the quilt? And with you two?"

"Oh, so now you're asking for a twofer? I don't know

that you're entitled to all of those answers."

Harper grabbed the newspaper that she'd set down nearby and rapped her friend on the head. "Lest we forget, it's me you're talking to. You know I'm not going to let this go."

Georgie held up her hands. "Fine. Okay. So no, I did not give him the quilt."

"Why not?"

She winced. "We got a little busy."

"Busy? Last I knew you two were barely talking."

"Yeah, but I guess when you disappeared I found out you weren't coming back anytime soon, and well you and I had promised to leave as soon as we could, so I told Spencer I was ready to leave and he insisted on making sure I got back safely."

"And?"

"Well, I had to invite him in. That would have been rude not to, don't you think? And then we had a drink. And we got to talking. And I realized I hadn't had sex in two years. And I got worried it had all petrified. And I figured he was as good a one-night stand as anyone, so why not put it all on black and hope for the best?"

Harper started to laugh. "You had a hookup? Sweet, innocent Georgie Childress did the nasty with a near stranger?"

Georgie playfully smacked at her hands. "You don't have to make it sound so tawdry. I mean it was practically one of those Kevin Bacon situations."

Harper lifted her eyebrows. "Kevin Bacon?"

"Yeah, you know how everyone knows everyone and we can all be connected to Kevin Bacon with six degrees of separation?"

"Okay…"

"I figured I know you and you know Noah and Noah knows Spencer, so it's not like we were complete strangers. Besides, I did hit his car."

"And kill his board."

"Rub it in, why don't ya."

Harper rubbed her hands. "This is so awesome. Georgie, I'm so happy for you. You broke the spell!"

"Don't get too excited. It was a one-off. The good news, is things didn't petrify down there."

"What's the bad news?"

"Did I say there was bad news?"

"No, but your face did."

"The bad news is I had a lot of fun. And he's slightly incredible in bed. I wasn't even sure about that man bun thing, either, but I found it sexy. Especially when he was—" She waved her hand as if to erase her comment.

"Go on."

Georgie shook her head. "Seriously, I've said far too much. Suffice it to say he does wonders with that mouth of his."

"Well, then you're going to have to find a way to have another date with that mouth of his."

"From your lips to his ears."

"Consider it done."

Chapter Fifteen

SPENCER was feeling a bit weird. Like he'd done something wrong when he knew he hadn't. They'd had a deal: it was only supposed to be a one-time fling. Testing the waters to make sure everything was still in working order. Proving to her that she could do way better than that Dan the Dick guy. Mission accomplished. So why did he feel like he was the big dick?

Maybe because he actually liked the crazy surfboard killer. Even if she had killed his board. But if she hadn't, then they'd never have met, and they'd never have slept together. And he'd never know what she tasted like, only to now find that he was craving that taste again and was disappointed that wasn't to be.

Of course he could reach out to her. But what would that accomplish? He didn't trust women after his girlfriend had betrayed him by letting his dad pay her off. No thanks. He wasn't interested in dealing with that type of nonsense. It was fine to get laid when the need presented itself and not get all tied up in knots with the complications that regularly came along with dating your average woman.

It had been a long day at work. When it grew cold this time of year, it was brutal trying to keep your hands warm enough to grip the steering wheel of the bike. Twice he'd had to swerve to avoid being hit by some jackass driver who wasn't paying attention. He was late with one delivery and got chewed out even though it wasn't his fault—his boss gave it to him and told him it had to be there in ten minutes, but the destination was a thirty-minute ride away.

Fuck it. He stood and went to the fridge and grabbed a beer.

He plunked down on his leather sofa and started to think. He went to set his beer down, and it made him ponder the idea she'd mentioned—about turning the dead board into something new. Repurposing it: end tables would look pretty sweet in here. He stood up, went out to the workshop, and removed the shroud that had been covering Petie since the accident. He found it didn't still feel quite so raw. Even though his baby was no longer, he only felt good memories for it. Maybe playing around with the raw edges, figuring out how to finish them off, putting the two halves onto a pedestal could work.

If nothing else, it would give him something to distract himself from the overarching feeling that, at the very least, he had been a real asshole to leave before saying goodbye.

Good thing he told her he wasn't one to stick around. He figured that might be all the harder for her, considering what happened the last time she counted on a man to not leave. At least she knew from the get-go it wasn't going to be that sort of relationship.

Now if he could only convince himself.

Falling for Mr. Maybe

There weren't many surfers in the water by early December. Even with his top-of-the-line wet suit, it was cold out there. When that water splashed on your face, it was a bracing smack of reality. But for Spencer, he was most at peace when he was on the water, alone with his thoughts. It was his place to meditate, and he hated to give it up for a few degrees of added comfort. Well, maybe more than a few.

He'd given himself enough time for about thirty minutes before the sun would set on him, and sure enough that final ride in took him to shore right as the sun went down.

He dragged his board out of the water and grabbed his stuff that he'd stashed farther up the beach, away from the tide. He draped an oversized fleece blanket around his shoulders and tucked his board under his armpit as he headed toward the parking lot. As he approached the dunes, he saw someone walking with a little dog. Passing her, he nodded and realized it was Georgie. "So, you're a dog person after all?"

Georgie looked up and gave a cursory nod. "Oh, hey Spencer. Fancy meeting you here." She continued walking, not even stopping to chat.

Spencer turned to follow her toward the beach, where he'd come from. "Uh, is there something wrong?"

She shook her head. "No. Why would there be?"

"Well, for starters, because you're ignoring me as if I'm a complete stranger."

She continued walking, letting the dog lead the way. "Well, you sort of are."

He tossed his head back, incredulous. "Not exactly," he said, walking quickly to catch up with her. He dropped his board so he could pick up the pace. Damn, she was going at a fast clip. "I mean, after all, I did have the pleasure of having my cock buried deep inside of you not too long ago. And we did exchange plenty of body fluids."

Georgie turned and tugged on the dog's leash so it would stop. "Yeah, so nothing new for you, am I right? I'm taking a page from your book. The last thing I want to be is some pity fuck of yours, so I've figured out how to be as uncaring about having sex with strangers as you have."

"Pity fuck? Is that what you think that was? A pity fuck?"

She shrugged. "I have no idea what it was. But if I had to bet money, I'd say that was exactly your intention."

He was freezing his ass off out here and needed to get inside his car with the heat blasting. But he wasn't going to leave this hanging.

"Look, you knew that I don't do relationships. I told you that. It's not in my repertoire. But that doesn't at all diminish what we shared."

He looked up to see tears glistening in her eyes. Oh, no. He knew what that meant. Shit.

"Unilaterally making it a one-night stand cheapens it. Because I wasn't worthy of you considering anything more than that." And then bam! Cue the failing floodgates. Tears started streaming down her face. And her dog—was it her dog? Or was she merely dog sitting for someone? He didn't even know enough about her to know if that was the case—started jumping up, his paws on her chest. Which made him mad that the dog was entitled to stick his paws on her tits yet he couldn't. But he couldn't because that was his decision, so he needed to stop thinking that way. The dog started licking at her face, but watching the swipes of that dog tongue catching her tears as they cascaded down her cheeks, he couldn't help but think he should be the one dabbing at them, not the damned dog.

"Look, Georgie," he said, extending his arms toward her. "I'd hug you, but I'm sopping wet and cold as hell. What say we at least sit in my car and discuss this? I can put on something warmer. And besides, you don't even have a jacket on and you're going to catch your death out here."

But Georgie shook her head. "There's nothing to say." She tugged gently on the dog's leash. "Come on, Bruiser. We need to get you back and get you fed."

And with that, she turned and walked away from Spencer, leaving him chilled to the bone for more reason than one.

Chapter Sixteen

GEORGIE couldn't console herself. Her sobs grew louder and even she knew they were getting ridiculous.

"Why am I not good enough for any man?" she cried to Margie as Bruiser finished gobbling down his dinner. *Typical male, selfishly inhaling a meal while a damsel in distress was nearby.* Note to self: when you get your own dog, be sure to get a female. She'd been pet sitting Bruiser for a woman she'd met at the gym, and while he was a sweet boy, Georgie was finding she wasn't interested in having any sort of male in her life. Even a canine version. She held her phone to her shoulder while she opened a bottle of wine. It was that kind of evening.

"Sweetie, you know this has nothing to do with you," Margie said. "It's clearly this man's problem. So why don't you try to accept that it's beyond your control. You had a nice time with him, chalk it up to life experience. And look at it this way: he taught you that Danny was even less impressive than you ever realized. That means you have a lot to look forward to in your next relationship."

Georgie bawled even louder, so much so she almost choked. "But why am I not good enough? Why can't he see that we truly connected? Why can't he try it on for size?"

"Because he probably can't. It's not in his genetic

makeup. And no amount of trying on your end will change that. I think the best thing you can do is move on, and if you run into him somewhere, say hello, talk about the weather, and be done with it."

"But what about the quilt?" Georgie said, gasping for air between huge sobs.

"Oh honey, that darned quilt. You should enjoy it yourself and don't even dream of giving it to him."

"Except now every time I see it, I'll think of him. And it'll make me cry all over again."

"That is quite the dilemma." Margie paused for a moment. "How about you tuck it away in your closet. Give it some time. I'm certain you'll eventually look at that quilt and won't even know why you made it to begin with. Problem solved. Case closed."

"But I want to have sex with him again." Georgie was certain the off switch for her tears was completely broken at this point, and she would ultimately cry herself into a state of dehydration and blow away like a dried, dead leaf. "I'm going to be old soon. And no man will want to sleep with me then."

"Don't be silly, Georgie. There's always Tinder."

"How do you know about Tinder?"

"Sweetie. I'm a sixty-year-old woman with needs. Believe me, there are plenty of men you can find on Tinder if push comes to shove."

"I can't believe my own mother's best friend is hooking up willy-nilly and I'm not."

Margie burst out laughing. "Willy-nilly? I suppose you could say it was that frivolous. But it's more like every now and then you need the satisfaction that only a man can give."

Georgie wailed. "And now that I've found out about

that, I won't experience it ever again."

"I promise you, you will, baby. But now I want you to get yourself to bed and stop your tears or the neighbors are going to think someone is beating on you."

Georgie's sobs were finally dying down. "I'm sorry. I didn't know who to call."

"Well, I hope you always know who to call. I'll always be here for you, baby doll. Good night!"

"G'nite, Margie. Thanks for taking such good care of me."

"Always, hon."

Georgie fell asleep with Bruiser draped across her stomach. At some point numbness set in, but she was too sound asleep to even notice.

She woke in the morning to a text from Marcy of all people.

Hey Georgie! We're having a few people over to our new place for a Christmas gathering. Hope you can make it.

Huh. Weird. Since when did Marcy want to extend hospitality toward her? Should she politely decline? Or show up and be gracious? What if it was some cruel joke, a setup by her Aunt Jeannie trying to exact revenge for the vibrator thing. She wouldn't put it past her.

She typed back a quick reply.

Sure. I'd love to.

She was nothing if not a good liar for the cause.

Chapter Seventeen

GEORGIE threw on her winter coat and gave Bruiser a few last pets goodbye before leaving for work.

"Now behave yourself and don't get into trouble."

She worried that a dog named Bruiser would be a four-legged disaster, but so far, he'd been sweet and kind, except for the bit about eating versus helping her to lick her wounds when she was on the phone with Margie. She guessed everyone had their shortcomings, and evidently his was his stomach.

She could relate. Her stomach was growling the entire drive to work, so she naturally had to make a quick stop at Hansen's doughnuts for a little breakfast pick-me-up. Besides, they had the best coffee in town.

She pulled into a space out front, leaving the car running so it would stay warm, and raced inside for two glazed doughnuts.

"Morning, Mrs. Hansen," she said with a smile.

"Georgie! So nice to see you bright and early. You all ready for the holidays?"

Georgie glanced around to see the place had practically vomited Christmas—decorations were thick and plentiful, and Bing Crosby was yammering on about holly and ivy or something on the stereo. Georgie didn't like to discuss it, but she'd given up on the Christmas spirit since Danny left. After all, they'd planned a holiday wedding, and when that all went to shit, well, so did her holiday cheer; they were inextricably tied.

She hated that, because she used to love Christmastime: the cozy, warm vibe of it, the cheesy music, the decorations, the parties. The mistletoe. Now? Well, who the hell would she kiss under the mistletoe in her place except Bruiser? And he was only there for a week. And she didn't need a plant-based prompt to give him a big hug and a kiss—she simply did it.

Nah, she'd leave it to the Mrs. Hansens of the world to maintain that Ho-ho-ho thing. She was over the false joy of the season; she was a pragmatist now.

"Not much getting ready for me, I suppose," she said. It went without saying that she didn't have a mom, she'd written off her dad long ago, and she sure as hell didn't have a man. If anything, Christmas rubbed her nose in her lack of close family.

"Did you put your tree up yet?" Mrs. Hansen wasn't taking the hint, so Georgie figured she'd have to lie to shut her up.

"Oh, yeah. It's a big one. Douglas fir. Must be nine feet tall with the star on top."

Mrs. Hansen whistled. "I bet it's a beaut."

Georgie nodded. Sometimes it worried her how good she was at lying. At least these were friendly white lies and wouldn't be hurtful to a soul. But for maybe herself. "Yep. Nothing like the holidays to lift your spirits up."

She asked for her doughnuts and coffee and shifted back and forth to try to warm up while she waited.

"I hear your cousin's got some extra special holiday news to share."

"Marcy?"

"You mean she didn't tell you?"

Georgie squinted her eyes. "Tell me?"

"About the little one on the way?" Mrs. Hansen poured the coffee into a to-go cup. "Leave room for cream?"

Georgie shook her head. "All the way to the top, please. I need all the fuel I can get to stay awake this early. So, you were saying?"

"Sorry. Didn't mean to spoil the surprise. Seems Marcy got married right in time, now that she has a bun in the oven."

Bun in the oven… Wow, that was fast. She was barely married a couple of weeks. Can you even tell that quickly if you get pregnant, say, on your honeymoon? That information was not in her wheelhouse, being that to date, she'd only spent her life avoiding being pregnant rather than calculating due dates. Being married and encouraging the process was a foreign concept to her.

"Yeah. Well. Wow. How exciting for them."

"Here are your doughnuts, hon. Now don't tell anyone you heard it from me. Maybe that was meant to be kept a secret."

More like Aunt Jeannie wanted to flaunt it when she sprang the news on Georgie. Her fertile daughter, naturally, who would have perfect blond-haired, blue-eyed babies who'd sleep through the night and never spit up and have perfect IQs and go to Harvard. Ugh.

By the time Georgie got to work, she couldn't stem the flow of tears that always seemed to hold her hostage at times like this. Damned tears. Why couldn't they go bother someone else and leave her the hell alone?

She sat in her car for a minute finishing her second doughnut—she'd gobbled the first one down faster than ole Bruiser had his dinner last night—and trying to tamp down the tears enough to go into the store without looking like someone had run over her dog.

Finally she felt like she looked presentable enough and entered the store. Only to find Harper and Noah canoodling by the cash register. Well, crap. If Noah was here at this hour, it meant that they'd come in together. And if they came in together, that meant they'd spent the night together. And if they spent the night together, that meant Georgie was the only woman on the planet who wasn't getting it on with a man, dammit.

It wasn't like she hadn't tried, but she'd tried with the wrong man, which was unfortunate. No matter how she tried, she found herself yearning for him. She liked the way his smile curled up more on one side of his face than the other. Besides the crooked smile, she liked that he was so easygoing. Not many men would have taken in stride what she'd done to his board without at least screaming some invectives her way or punching a window.

But maybe it was a sign: if she could find some

happiness in Spence's company, then surely there were other men out there whose company she could enjoy. But what were the chances she'd find one who was so skillful at pleasuring a woman? Danny had proven that such abilities weren't a given. Which meant she was going to be relegated to a lifetime of vibrators, and no more dancing tongues to bring her to a climax like no other.

Well, poop. Those tears were surfacing again.

"Morning, Georgie!" Noah said, enveloping her in a big bear hug. Going forward, it was likely the only hug she'd ever get from a man, and that made her even sadder.

"Hey, Noah," she said, her shoulders sagging as she set her coffee on the display case.

"Are you crying?" Harper said, scurrying over to give her friend a hug. "What's wrong?"

Georgie's shoulders heaved as a long, large sob released itself from her body. She'd tried so hard to hold it in, but sometimes those tears had a will of their own.

"Nothing," she said between gasps.

"Well of course there's something," her friend said. "You don't simply show up for work and start bawling." She looked at Georgie's face, dusting off glazed doughnut icing from the corners of her mouth. "Are you mad at yourself because you ate doughnuts?"

Georgie's eyes opened wide. "How do you know I had doughnuts? And no! Why would I be?"

Harper held out her hands in despair. "I don't know. I was only taking a stab in the dark to try to figure out why you are so blue."

"It's December!" Georgie said as a flood of tears descended yet again. That short sentence should be all anyone needed to know if they wanted to learn why Georgie was so upset.

Chapter Eighteen

"OH, honey. I'm sorry. I should have realized." She glanced at the calendar on the wall—one of those freebie calendars with kitty cats on it in seasonal attire. The December picture had three kittens asleep with miniature Santa Claus hats on their tiny heads. They were perfectly adorable. Georgie knew those kitties had lots of people—and kitties—to love them in their lives and that made her cry even more. "It would have been next week, right?"

Noah raised his hand, obviously in the dark. "Uh, what would have been next week?"

"My wedding." Georgie bawled, even though she knew that every man worth his salt squirmed and trembled at the sight of a crying woman. She didn't care. He was a man, and a man was to blame for her tears so he needed to man up and take credit for the rest of them. Inevitably they all were to blame at some point for breaking a woman's heart, so there should be some sort of collective guilt owned by their half of the species.

"Oh, crap," he said. "You were supposed to get married next week? But I thought you and Spencer recently hooked up—" He pointed a finger at her and then toward the outside, the finger evidently aiming toward where Spencer lived.

Harper kicked him. "Ix-nay on encer-spay," she said.

"What?" he said half under his breath to Harper as if Georgie couldn't hear him. Of course she could, even past her continued crying fits.

"Georgie was engaged to be married a few years ago, and her cad of a fiancé skipped out on her weeks before the big day."

Yep, that was Georgie's life in a nutshell.

"Oh, Georgie, I'm really sorry. I had no idea."

She held her hand up to dismiss it. "It's fine." She reached for the nearby tissues and took the whole box, as one or two would not suffice under the circumstances.

"And the subject of Spencer isn't helping matters, so let's not discuss him either," Harper said, elbowing Noah. He held his hands up in surrender. Clearly the females confounded him. "Right, sweetie?"

Georgie nodded. The last thing she wanted to do was talk about Spencer, the commitment-phobic commitment-phobe. And yet she couldn't stop herself. "What's the matter with me? Why won't he even try to see if we could be more than fuck buddies? Not that we are fuck buddies. That was a one-time thing. And I should be ashamed of myself for capitulating like I did but you know what? I'm perfectly fine with it. I needed a good shagging, to quote Austin Powers. It had been way too long since I'd had honest-to-goodness sex with a man. And longer still since I'd had exceptional honest-to-goodness sex with a man." She shrugged. "Who knew? Here I thought sex with all men was the same. I mean Danny was pretty perfunctory: you're in, you're out. You get what I mean? But Spencer—wowza. That man has a magical tongue. And I think we can leave it at that because what he did to me with that tongue was downright spiritual. I probably came six times that night."

"Georgie—are you sure you want to get into such detail with Noah here?"

"Why should I care anymore? My sex life is over and done with. I might as well look back on the high points with reverie, right? After all, it's what is going to take me into my dotage. Me thinking back to the good old days—make that day—better yet, night—when Spencer—oh God, what is his last name? I'm not even sure what his last name is. Does that make me super slutty that I slept with a guy whose last name escapes me—if I ever even knew it? Anyhow, when Spencer What's-His-Name gave me a Big O with his mouth." She looked skyward, as if toward the angels, remembering fondly the moment when. "Have you ever done that?" She pointed at Noah, who was turning red with embarrassment.

Harper put her arm over her shoulder. "Sweetie, a good man totally does that. In fact, for future reference, now that you've experienced it, be sure to only go with a guy who has that tool in his tool chest, so to speak."

"But there won't be another guy," she wailed. "I'm relegated to that damned vibrator for all of eternity. I need to give it a name. Like some sexy Italian name. Alfredo. It's me and Alfredo for life. At least Alfredo won't betray me. Or slip out the door at five in the morning. There's something to be said for the steadfastness of a rechargeable machine. Besides, if Alfredo eventually dies—from overuse, no doubt—I can always replace him, no questions asked. No feelings hurt."

"Why don't I step out and grab a couple more doughnuts," Noah said, his eyebrows ski-sloped in a plea to flee.

"That would be amazing if you could do that," Harper

said. "And I'll stay here and soothe my friend Georgie's soul."

It was all fine and good for them both to help out—because to be truthful, Georgie could sit and eat a dozen doughnuts right now in an attempt to self-soothe—but she was fairly certain that nothing was going to do much to appease her still-fragile heart.

Chapter Nineteen

"DUDE," Noah said over coffee and doughnuts with Spencer. "What the fuck did you do to Georgie? I mean, I asked you to be my wingman and all, and thanks for that, but shit, she's a hot damned mess and a puddle of tears. I couldn't get out of there fast enough this morning because I sure as hell didn't know what to say to her. And I had the impression it was all thanks to you."

Spencer shook his head as he took a sip of his coffee, which he promptly spat out. "Crap, that was hot," he said. "Burned my damned mouth."

"Here. Have a doughnut. I've been eating them for half an hour now, in fear of returning to the shop but knowing I promised I'd bring some of these back."

"Yeah, well I'm gonna get an earful when I show up late for work this morning too." He grabbed a blueberry doughnut and popped a chunk of it in his mouth.

"So, what the hell man? First off, I guess you deserve props because apparently you've got the best damned tongue in the state of North Carolina."

Spence looked up from blowing on his coffee. "Huh?"

"In between all the tears and moaning and groaning—"

Spencer held up his hand to pause his friend, taking a

moment to flash back to the moaning and groaning he remembered all too acutely.

"As I was saying, in between all the moaning and groaning, she kept talking about your masterful tongue, so I guess there's that."

Spencer shook his head. "She'd been telling me what a dud that ex of hers was. I challenged her that there were plenty of good guys out there, and lots and lots of good— make that great—sex. I told her it was all just a friends thing though. That I don't do relationships. That I wasn't interested in anything more than a fling."

"Have you ever met a woman on the planet who seriously believed that?"

"About good guys and good sex?"

"No. About the commitment-free fuck."

He shrugged. "Actually I've met a bunch. That's the beauty of hookup apps."

Noah erased the air with his hands. "Apart from them. Like legit women looking for legit connections with a guy. Not that the other ones aren't legit, but they have different needs they're trying to meet. But a woman like Georgie is decidedly not that type of gal. Georgie is not the one who would seek a one-night stand."

"How do you know that?"

Noah threw him some shade. "Well, let's see. She wears sensible shoes. Have you ever met a hookup on Tinder who was in sensible shoes?"

Spencer laughed, thinking back to any of those women, and pretty much their footwear involved spiked heels. "Good point. What else?"

"She drives a beat-up Volvo that's about a thousand years old. Not your typical hookup vehicle."

"True."

"Oh. And she quilts. She even made you a quilt! What woman who's looking for a one-night stand does that?"

Spencer squinted at him. "What do you mean she made me a quilt?"

"You didn't see the thing? Harper told me all about it. After she broke your board she felt so bad about it she wanted to make you an apology gift. But she didn't even know who you were or where you lived. So, she decided to make this damned quilt in case she happened to run into you again—figuratively not literally, I'm supposing."

"Yeah, definitely no more running into me like that." He paused as he tried his coffee again. This time it was mercifully cool enough to drink without scalding the roof of his mouth. "But you know I did run into her last night. And it didn't go well. She was obviously mad at me—she pretended we hardly knew each other. When I called her out on it she got angrier and then she stormed off."

"That would be the reaction of a woman who makes quilts for strangers whose boards she destroys. Not the reaction of a woman looking for a quick night of hot sex with the hopes of never seeing the dude again."

Spencer thrust his lower lip out in a frown. "Shit."

Noah nodded. "Yup."

"So, what am I supposed to do with this information?"

Noah shook his head. "Hell if I know. That's for you to sort out. But I wanted you to know that you didn't do Georgie any favors by pegging her as one of those girls who didn't care."

"But she said herself she wasn't looking for anything serious—" Wait, had she said that? Or was he conveniently remembering that? Because in the heat of the moment, talk switched from him not wanting serious relationships to her putting her hand on his thigh and then the next thing he knew they were naked and he'd lost all semblance of thinking clearly. Had she, in fact, talked about that, or had he assumed as much? "Awww, crap. I'm such a dickhead."

Noah lifted his eyebrow. "Tell me something I don't already know." He grinned.

"I was so busy talking to her about how I didn't go for relationships, I never even bothered to be sure that wasn't what she was looking for. Which wasn't all that fair of me, was it?"

"She made you a freaking quilt. I don't know much about things like that except that what Harper said is it takes a ton of time to make. It's not something you whip together in twenty minutes like an omelet."

Spencer of all people understood what handcrafting something meant. It was a labor of love as much as anything else. Not that Georgie loved him, but she cared enough about him and his feelings and how she'd hurt and upset him to go to such lengths? What woman does that?

But he already had the answer to his rhetorical question: the kind of woman who a man should want to explore a deepening relationship with. Not the kind who would accept money from an asshole father to try to woo you back into the family fold. This is a woman who sacrificed her time and care for someone she didn't even know. Yet. And now she knew him in a way that made her feel special. Until he made it clear that wasn't the case on his end.

Sometimes it's easy to learn life lessons, and other times you need to be bashed over the head with the truth to soak it in. This was one of those times. He needed to figure out how to fix what he broke here, which was, most unexpectedly, this sweet woman's heart.

Chapter Twenty

"THE thing is, I knew he went into this thing with the understanding it was a one-night stand. He told me as much. So I wasn't ignorant about it. And I told myself I was merely going to tap into the irrigation system that had suddenly made itself available to me to end my dry spell... turn that hose on full blast." She grinned through her tears.

"I'm glad you can laugh at it at least."

"Yeah well, if you don't laugh, you cry."

"I'm sorry, Georgie. I wish I could help you."

"The thing is, I know I'm as much at fault as he is—if there is fault to be assigned to anyone here. I made an impulsive decision to go for it. I knew I wasn't keen on the whole notion of having impersonal sex. But, well, it had been so long. He was there. He seemed nice. He was cute. He promised me it would be exceptional. And he didn't lie about that, either, but I didn't realize that having sex with him was going to trigger some need for emotional connection with the guy. I thought I was totally over the whole emotion thing with men. After Danny, I closed myself off so much I didn't think I'd ever be able to open up that way for any man. I figured I'd be fine."

"But you're not."

Georgie shook her head. Her tearstained face felt tight

to the touch, her hopes and dreams shriveled up like her parched face. Her foolish wish that maybe she and Spencer could explore some sort of relationship together, completely shot down.

"I'm going to be frank with you, now, honey. It's for your own good." Harper took a deep breath. "You've got to pull yourself together. No man is worth falling to pieces over, Georgie. You're a strong, smart, adorably charming, vibrant young woman. You might think you're never going to find another man again, but I promise you, you will. And he's going to be the man you deserve, someone who will love and cherish you—"

"And have an amazing tongue?"

She laughed, nodding. "Yes, that too. The whole package. And the timing will be right and you'll be ready for him and he'll be ready for you and you'll be glad you held out hope for that perfect Mr. Right."

"But what if Mr. Maybe seemed to be perfect already?"

Her friend shrugged. "If he wasn't willing to sacrifice for you, then he wasn't perfect enough for you. I don't want you to settle for anything less, and I also don't want you to abandon all hope that someday, you'll find yourself in a relationship that you deserve."

Georgie wiped her eyes again and fixed her gaze on Harper's. "You think so? You don't think I'm officially yesterday's trash?"

Harper laughed. "Goodness, no. You're the most untrashy woman I know."

"I guess that's a compliment."

Harper hugged her. "In the best sense of the word. You're one in a million, Georgie. And don't you forget it."

The minute Spencer left work for the day, he hightailed it to his workshop and got down to business. He'd been mulling ways to implement Georgia's brilliant idea for repurposing his dead board. And he finally figured out a way to do it. After trimming away and sanding down the raw edges where the board had once been one, he carefully cut two thin bands of wood, which he applied with a strong epoxy along the edge of each piece of the board. Sure only one edge of the "table" was going to have that band along it, but it would then fit nicely against the wall next to the sofa as if that was part of the design all along.

On his way home from work he'd stopped at the hardware store and purchased two solid granite pedestals, which he secured to the underside of the board pieces with metal brackets. And while he distracted himself with this project, he mulled over what a prick he'd been to poor Georgie, who totally didn't deserve to be treated like she was disposable. Because no matter how you looked at it, that was the message he'd sent to her and was no different from the message Douchebag Dan had given her as well. He was no better than that dickhead, and he hated himself all the more for it.

The question now was how could he get himself back into Georgie's good graces? It was obvious she would avoid him at all costs. She could easily pretend their little fling was meaningless, but he knew better. And he owed it to her to fix this.

Chapter Twenty-One

HO *ho ho and all that crap.* That's what Georgie was thinking as she got ready for this little Christmas bash at Marcy's. Make that Marcy and James's. Or would that be Jameses'? She never knew how to do that. Make that Marcy and James's and the alleged Baby Marcy-and-James. How weird was that? She tried to do the math on when the baby was due, but she wasn't clear on when doctors date the pregnancy—at the point of conception? But who knew when that was? Or once you're confirmed pregnant? Would she be due next fall? She counted on her fingers, figuring if she was pregnant mid-November, then maybe mid-August? Well, she'd be schvitzing that out next summer for sure—nine months pregnant in the dead heat of a North Carolina summer? No thank you, ma'am.

Georgie figured if she were ever to have a baby, it would, at this point, need to be both immaculate conception and immaculate delivery. She wanted that thing out with no muss, no fuss. She saw those scary videos of babies being delivered in health class and that made her skin crawl. Like who would invent such a barbaric procedure?

A man. That's who. Typical.

As much as Georgie wasn't keen on being all flush

with holiday spirit, she did like a cute holiday dress, and a few years ago she had found an adorable, short, royal-blue scoop-necked sweaterdress tastefully trimmed in fake fur. It looked like something Mrs. Claus might wear on a date. A little spicy, emphasizing her best asset, her breasts, and her second-best asset, her legs. She donned a pair of sexy silver sandals, stuck two small Christmas ornament earrings in her ears, threw on her coat, and left, grabbing the obligatory bottle of wine for the hostess from the kitchen on her way out. She had half a mind to give Marcy one of those lousy, lamentable bottles of re-gifted wine people sometimes show up with. She never knew what to do with those and so far had donated them to the local food drive. Though that was likely not what they had meant when they said food drive. Instead she grabbed one of her better bottles, thinking it's what she'd want someone to do for her.

She parked a block away, realizing too late the sandals she'd put on were look-don't-walk shoes. Her feet were already hurting by the time she arrived at their door.

James greeted her at the entrance with a kiss and took her coat, pointing toward the kitchen, where Marcy was. The house was Christmased out in a big way—they must have bought out the holiday décor section at Target.

"Am I early?" she asked James. A cursory look revealed that she was the only one there.

"No." He shook his head. "Didn't Marc tell you? It's only a small dinner thing."

"Oh gosh, sorry. I thought it was a big blowout. I mean why else would I be invited?" She covered her mouth the minute she said that, knowing it might sound snide.

James put his arm around Georgie's shoulder. "Because Marcy likes you. That's why. And so do I."

Okay, then… That was weird. Was she in the alternate universe in which her cousin was her friend? How supremely unexpected!

Georgie walked into the kitchen. "Georgie! So great to see you!" Her cousin enveloped her in a big hug.

"Hey!" Georgie said, plastering on a less-than-heartfelt smile. "How was your honeymoon?"

"It was fabulous," her cousin said as she started to rub her belly. "Though I guess you could also call it a babymoon."

Georgie cocked her head and squinted. "Babymoon?"

James joined them in the kitchen and put his arm around his new wife. "We've got some great news to share with you."

Oh God. This was it. They were going to tell her about the baby due next fall and she was going to have to fake it and pretend she was none the wiser.

"Yeah? What is it?"

Marcy pulled something off of her refrigerator and handed it to her cousin. "This. It's our sonogram picture. We're having a baby in April!"

Georgie did a quick head shake. April? Huh? That would be the shortest gestation period in the history of— wait a minute. She did some quick mental math. That means she was pregnant well before she got married. Like even before she got engaged in September. And they did get married awfully quickly, come to think of it. Everyone said they were simply so excited to be husband and wife.

"A baby! You guys! You sure made fast work of it!"

"Well, not that fast," she said. "If you do the math you can figure out we were expecting well before we got married."

Gee, really? "Oh. I hadn't thought about that. I don't

usually think about things like babies I guess."

Marcy put her hand on her shoulder. "I'm sorry, Georgie. I need to apologize to you. I was so wrapped up in my own world that I have never reached out to you to tell you how bad I felt for how Dan treated you. To be honest, I don't think you deserved him, and I was glad when he was out of the picture."

Georgie knit her brows. "What do you mean?"

"Like that time at my mother's sixtieth birthday party when you two came down here. Remember that?"

Yeah, she remembered it. Her aunt seemed not particularly thrilled that Georgie showed up, a fiancé in tow. She figured it was because she was going to beat her daughter to the altar. It was Jeannie's way.

"Well, that weekend I was out with some girlfriends at Catfish's. We were all drinking and whooping it up. And Dan came in and started chatting up my friends as if he had every right to do that. He was buying drinks for one of them, even took her phone number. I was shocked by it. But then I guess I hoped he'd buckle down and get serious once you two were married."

Huh. So, this was news. Danny was seen in public coming on to other women when they were engaged? And no one even told her?

"The thing is, Georgie, I need to apologize for my mother's bad behavior too. I guess until recently I hadn't seen her for all the ugly reality of it. And not to excuse it, but I guess she was jealous of you, since you were going to be married before I was. Stupid behavior, and she's way too old for it."

Georgie shrugged. "Thanks. Yeah, your mom never did like me much."

James handed Georgie a tall glass of wine and a

sparkling water to his wife.

"I don't think it's that she doesn't like you so much as she doesn't like herself. That might be the armchair psychologist in me, but honestly, my mother needs to get a life. She's far too busy meddling in others' lives and not at all concerned about how she comes across."

Georgie was trying to figure out how to agree 150 percent with her cousin without coming across as insulting.

"The fact is my mother should have brought you under her wing when your mother died, but instead it was like she doubled down on you. It was all too much with this wedding. And to be honest, I have been so freaking exhausted and sick as a damned dog, I didn't have it in me to deal with it, but I wanted to. I was up to my eyeballs in my own stupid stuff."

Georgie nodded, taking it all in. This rewriting of history had taken her by complete surprise.

"You want to know a secret?"

Well, hell. Georgia couldn't imagine what secrets were still left after all of this gut-spilling.

"When you said that thing to my mother at that bridal shower, I about peed my pants. I knew I couldn't burst out laughing or my mother would freak out on me, but oh my God. Trust me, I was high-fiving you inside and laughing my ass off. Did you see my mother actually spluttered?

"Heh. Her little tea sandwich dropped right out of her mouth."

"Yes! The stupid cucumber sandwich, which no one in their whole life would ever crave. And here she is stuffing that in her piehole, and you drop the bomb about your vibrators. It's a wonder I didn't wet my pants, what with this pregnancy and me peeing all the time anyhow."

Georgie stood there, taking sips of her wine in rapid

succession, not knowing exactly how she should respond.

"Gee, Marcy. I have to admit this all comes as a bit of a surprise. I mean your mother, yeah. She's not my biggest fan, and I never understood why. But I'm glad to know that I wasn't imagining it all at least."

"Oh, not hardly. And when I told her we were expecting she seemed appalled that we weren't married. I think her words were something along the lines of 'how dare you get knocked up?'"

Georgie scrunched her nose. Not a very maternal response there. "I'm sorry, Marc. I didn't realize she was that way to you too."

Marcy waved her hand. "Oh, she alternates between being passive-aggressive and being smothering and boastful of me toward others. I guess I'm so used to it I don't even react when she's like this toward others like you. And I do owe you an apology for that. Particularly because I think she was compensating toward you. Angry at me, throwing her wrath your way. It's the Jeannie way."

"I guess I should be all the more grateful that my mother wasn't at all like that when she was alive."

"Funny, isn't it? You had it great with your mother, and then she was taken away from you so early. And me, well, you see what I have to contend with. My mother hissed at me that we couldn't tell anyone about the baby or we'd arouse suspicions. I told her to stuff it—as soon as I was past the fear of miscarrying, I was happy to let the world know. We're excited and proud about our pregnancy, and it doesn't matter which came first, the pregnancy or the marriage. That's a relic of her ridiculously puritanical thought processes, not mine. She about birthed a cow when I said that."

She opened the oven door and pulled out a tray of

something she set on top of the stove. "She's so damned concerned about one-upping her dead sister even still, that she was mortified I would be pregnant before I was married. Meanwhile, I could give two cares. James and I love each other, we'll love our baby, and whether it was conceived in or out of wedlock is not anything I lose a moment's sleep over." She reached out and hugged Georgie, who felt the threat of tears. She closed her eyes and concentrated on not letting them spill. The last thing she needed was to be bawling at a dinner party with whatever stranger they'd invited to this meal.

Chapter Twenty-Two

GEORGIE was still suppressing her tears when the doorbell rang. Right in the nick of time.

"I'll get it, honey," James said.

Georgie was so awkward with confessionals, but she appreciated her cousin's candor. "Thanks, Marc. I know it wasn't easy for you to say those things to me, and I am grateful that you mustered up the courage."

Marcy waved her hand. "It was high time I did and I apologize for taking so long." She wiped her hands on a dishtowel. "Here—help me carry this stuff into the dining room." She handed her a big bowl of pasta tossed with shrimp and flecks of lemon and arugula and she carried the tray of garlic bread.

"Looks fantastic."

"Thanks! I was hoping you two would like it."

They walked into the dining room as James and Spencer turned the corner and entered the room. Georgie's eyes opened wider than one of those rain forest tree frogs. What the hell was he doing here?

"Georgie, I think you know Spencer, right? We saw you two talking at the wedding, and it looked like you were having a good time." Marcy extended her hands out to indicate the newest arrival. "And Spencer, you remember

Jenny Gardiner

Georgie, right?"

If only they knew that she did indeed know Spencer, in the biblical sense, at least. You could safely say they were quite biblically acquainted. Although one would wonder how the bible became linked with knowing someone sexually. Ugh, she had to stop thinking about sex when she thought of him. Because she started getting that tingly feeling there, and she knew what followed that. Before the salad course was done, her panties would be soaked. Which made her think about how he lapped her up the last time he made her so wet. She almost groaned, but luckily, she caught herself before doing that out loud, which would have been super embarrassing.

She nodded and placed the bowl of pasta on the table. "Oh, hey, Spencer." She hoped that would suffice, but hell, no. Spencer had to come over and reach out and give her a hug. A damned hug. So that their bodies were touching.

"It's great to see you, Georgie." He fixed his hazel eyes on hers and it was as though some laser had homed in on her soul. She mentally squirmed beneath his undivided attention.

"Um, yeah. This is quite a surprise to see you here." She paused, debating whether to get a dig in, then decided, what the hell. It was the holiday season, after all. The season for giving. She wondered if that also included giving someone crap. "I hadn't expected to see you ever again."

Spencer grinned. "Touché. But surely you didn't think you'd get rid of me that easily, now did you?"

She knit her brow. "Oh, I know perfectly well how to get rid of you in one fell swoop." All she had to do was sleep with him and express a hint of affection. That was all it took for him to vamoose out of there faster than a firewalker on flaming coals.

113

"Although more than likely there were extenuating circumstances that led you to make presumptions."

"Spence, how about I get you a glass of wine before we sit down?"

"Sure, that would be great."

Georgie was confused and feeling off-balance. First she came here for "true confessions" with Marcy, which was, after all, kind of nice and soul cleansing, and then *he* shows up? She couldn't figure out if this was some joke or a weird attempt at matchmaking after Marcy and James saw the two of them together at the wedding.

Marcy offered them each a seat across from one another, and it seemed almost like a showdown—as if she should be preparing for the gunfight with him at the O.K. Corral. Well, she was going to have to presume the best of everyone here—with, perhaps, the exception of Spencer—and proceed with dinner like a normal person. With no preconceived notions. And hope she wasn't being set up for some type of joke. But even that—Spencer might be a jerk, but he wasn't a mean person. So, no. That couldn't be what was behind this. Maybe it was simply four adults enjoying a dinner party?

James brought in the wine bottle and poured some for Spence and refilled Georgie's glass, then gave his bride some more sparkling water.

"Big downside to pregnancy—wine withdrawals," she said, looking down at her stomach. "This baby best appreciate the sacrifices I'm making on his or her behalf. Oh, and no sushi for the duration. Not to mention no hair highlights. The things we do for our children." She winked at her cousin. "Or to our children, as the case may be." They both laughed at that.

James held up his wineglass. "I just wanted to say

we're excited to have you both here for dinner—you're our first since we got married. We're so happy you could join us and here's to friends"—he nodded at Spencer—"family"—he tipped his head to Georgie"—and a wonderful holiday."

They raised their glasses and toasted.

James rubbed his hands together. "Now let's eat!" He passed the pasta to Georgie first, who gave herself a generous portion. She thought to apologize for it but then figured, fuck it. She was hungry. She handed it down to Marcy, and James passed the sautéed French green beans to her.

"So, I have to admit I was intrigued when I saw Spencer at work after we returned from the honeymoon, and he told me how you two had originally met."

Ahhh... so that was the connection. She didn't realize the two of them worked together.

She smiled one of those smiles you have to paste on your face when you'd rather spit on the ground. At Spencer. "Yeah, sort of a silly little accident."

"I'm glad I wasn't there to witness that because I suspect I would have seen a grown man cry. He loved that board so much."

"Yeah, well, the only crying that went on was poor Georgie."

"Georgie never met an occasion she didn't want to cry at," Marcy said. "Amiright?"

Georgie winced. "Okay, so it's true. I get a little emotional."

Spence arched his brow. "A little?"

Marcy and James gave each other a knowing look.

"What's that supposed to mean?" Georgie said.

Spencer shrugged. "It's only that I've seen you break

down a couple of times and it can get traumatic pretty quickly."

"Fine, so I'm an ugly crier."

"I think you're an adorable crier."

Georgie frowned. He wasn't entitled to think she cried adorably. He wasn't entitled to think anything about her whatsoever!

Out of nowhere, she felt something on her sandaled foot. She threw a subtle glance to the right and the left. Surely it wasn't one of them, trying to play footsies with each other and finding the wrong foot under the table.

She would simply ignore it and hope it would stop.

But it didn't. Five minutes later, as she was taking another bite of her shrimp, she felt the sock-clad foot slide up her shin, slip beneath her dress, and settle smack-dab between her legs, right *there*. He wouldn't.

He would.

She looked at him, but he didn't even glance her way. He was busily discussing some zoning issue with his boss while Marcy got up to replenish the pasta.

His toes insinuated their way along her center, and sure enough, that damned tingling sensation started up again, and moisture flooded her panties. Soon his toe was focusing its efforts on her clit, pressing and circling, and she had no choice but to spread her legs even more, because, well it felt pretty damned amazing. Before she knew it, his toes were insinuating their way beneath the edge of the leg of her panties, which meant there was no way he wouldn't realize the effect he was having on her, she was so wet. She tried to discreetly press herself against him, hoping her hosts hadn't a clue what was going on right beneath their dinner table. Even though at this point she could hardly care.

Except this was Spencer doing this and she'd washed her hands of him.

"Oh, Marcy, this pasta is amazing," Spencer said, not giving any indication of his other preoccupation down below.

"I'd love to get the recipe." Georgie was proud that she could focus enough to continue a conversation when in fact her body was screaming, "Recipe, schmecipe!"

"Of course, I'll email it to you."

"So, anyone have any big plans for the holidays?" James asked.

Georgie shook her head. "I don't really do Christmas, so I'll lay low, maybe do Chinese carryout."

"Georgie, you're welcome to come to our place," Marcy said. "Though on second thought, my mother isn't particularly gracious toward you, so I can't see why you would want that."

"It's fine. I'm happy pretending it's just another day." And even more fine pretending that Spencer wasn't trying to bring her to climax with his foot. Which he was having great success at attempting to do. Her breathing became sharper and her senses more acute. All the focus was on that place where he was applying the perfect amount of pressure. God, she wished his fingers were there as well. His mouth, for that matter.

"Spence, what about you?"

He poured some more wine into his glass, adding a splash more to both Georgie's and James's as well.

"I'm in the Georgie corner on this. I don't get into Christmas too much. After I moved away from home, well, it wasn't anything that came up in my day-to-day life."

James pointed at each of them and then crisscrossed his hands. "You two should spend it together. Sounds like you have the same attitude about it.

"What a great idea," Spencer said, finally making eye contact with her. His eyes twinkled, and he winked at her. She wasn't sure if that was a wink of collusion about what was happening beneath the table or sloughing off the Christmas suggestion. But she was sure she needed to stop this autoerotic manipulation that was happening. It was unseemly. Here her cousin was trying to be a nice hostess and she was busily trying to suppress any signs of an imminent orgasm.

Georgie wiped her mouth with a napkin. "If you'll excuse me for a second."

"Powder room is out of commission because it has a coat of fresh paint on it. Go on up the stairs and you'll find another bathroom, second door on the right," Marcy said.

As Georgie climbed the stairs, her legs rubbed together, and she feared she'd come right then and there from the delicious friction. She was going to take care of matters upstairs and get past it so she could proceed with her dinner in peace. All she needed was about thirty seconds and she'd be right back at the dinner table.

Chapter Twenty-Three

SPENCER was nursing a hard-on like nothing he'd experienced before. He had so enjoyed watching Georgie pretend nothing was happening when he knew she was so close to coming. He could see it in her pupils and the way she kept biting her lip. And then she up and excused herself to go to the bathroom. Either to tamp it down or rub it out herself. But he wasn't going to let her off that easily; he intended to finish what he'd started.

He slipped his foot back into his loafer, then set his napkin on the table. "I'll be right back," he said, trying to discreetly tug his black cashmere sweater down to hide how big his dick had grown in his pants.

He wasn't worried what James and Marcy would think about him following her to the bathroom—James was well-versed on the latest in the Georgie-Spencer saga. He was the one who helped facilitate this dinner to begin with. Besides, they were newlyweds. They knew the drill.

Stealthy as a cat, he climbed the stairs, hot on Georgie's heels. And when she turned the corner and stepped into the bathroom, he was able to wedge his foot in before she could even close the door.

She gasped, and he closed his hand over her mouth to not arouse suspicion. The only thing he wanted aroused right now was her. And maybe him.

But Georgie wasn't an easy one, and quickly bit down on his finger.

"Ouch!" he said. "What was that for?"

"That was for, well, it was for, everything."

"Everything?"

"Yes, like I said. Everything."

"Okay, but what happened to how much fun we were having?"

"That'll teach you to get a girl in a vulnerable position and toy with her like that."

He pulled her closer, so that his hard cock was pressed up against the notch at her thighs. "This'll teach you to get a guy in a vulnerable position as well."

"What is that supposed to mean?"

Spencer closed the bathroom door then hitched her leg up around him as he pressed his lips against hers, desperate to feel her tongue dueling with his again. He reached down with one hand and slid his fingers beneath the leg of her panties. She groaned. She was so slick, it made his pulse beat like mad. He needed to make her come and fast. Then he needed to come inside her. On her. Under her. But that would have to wait.

"That means that you, Georgie Childress, went and snuck under my skin when I wasn't looking."

"Kind of like how you snuck your fingers where they are when I wasn't looking."

"Do you want to look?"

She looked at him, then nodded. Christ, this is what he loved about her. She was open and honest and uninhibited. He pulled away from her while she held her dress up as they both watched him trace his fingers through her slick center.

"Oh God, Spencer, that feels so amazing."

He leaned down and bit her nipple through her dress. "I can't tell you how much I want you right now," he said. "But we're going to have to wait for that. For now, I'll have to settle on watching you watch yourself as I make you come."

Georgie thrust her hips against his hand, encouraging him to move faster. He slid two fingers inside her while the others worked her clit and he could feel the convulsions start inside of her as she let out a loud moan. He closed his mouth over hers to shush her before their hosts could hear them. "That's it, Georgie. Come for me, baby." It seemed ages but was only a minute later that Georgie stopped trembling and collapsed against Spence, his fingers still inside her.

"We need to get downstairs! They're going to wonder what happened to us."

Spencer figured they'd put two and two together by now. He pulled his fingers from her and licked them clean, sharing them with Georgie, who sucked on his pointer finger like she was toying with his cock. He groaned, then smacked her on her bottom.

"Let's get down there and finish this meal up so we can get back to business."

Georgie went ahead of Spencer, hoping her flushed face wasn't a dead giveaway.

"Everything okay up there?" Marcy arched her brow and grinned.

"Yes, fine."

"We thought we lost you two."

"You mean Spence? I didn't even know he was upstairs. I didn't even see him."

Marcy nodded. "Oh. Okay then."

When Spencer returned to the table, James rubbed his hands together. "Who's ready for dessert?"

Georgie took one look at Spencer and her eyes lit up. "I, for one, can't wait."

Chapter Twenty-Four

"THANKS for such an amazing evening," Georgie said. She gave her cousin a hug and this time she meant it. "I'm so happy for you two. And thanks for sharing everything with me."

Georgie and Spencer left in their own cars but met up a block away.

"My place. Follow me," Spencer said.

Georgie liked his take-charge demeanor. And she loved the way he could surprise her like he did at the dinner table.

After a ten-minute drive, they arrived at his place, a surprisingly large contemporary house on the beach.

Georgie followed him inside and into a cozy living room. The curtains were all opened wide. "I don't ever want to not see the ocean right there," he said, pointing toward the water. She nodded—she felt the same way.

"Before anything else, I need to show you something."

Georgie frowned, wondering what this could mean.

"Oh, it's nothing bad. It's something you deserve all the credit for, so I wanted you to be the first to have a glimpse at it."

He covered her eyes and guided her from behind. When he removed his hands, before her stood two familiar-looking end tables. "Ta-da!" he said with a grin.

She held her hand to her mouth. "Oh, wow. Petie! Doing business as a side table." She squealed and clapped her hands. "I love them! They're downright gorgeous!"

"And I have you to thank. In fact, I want you to have them. Courtesy of Broken Board Designs." He winked at her.

"Really? For me?"

He nodded. "Consider them an early Christmas present."

"I didn't know we were exchanging gifts this year. I thought we didn't even celebrate Christmas!"

"Well, I thought maybe now was a time for new beginnings. Starting with me, Spencer, finally admitting that you, Georgie, are someone I want to get to know better. Granted, we sort of got to know each other intimately before we got to know each other as friends, but I was hoping you'd agree that we could undertake a little bit of both and see where things lead."

She shook her head.

"No?" He frowned at her.

"No, not a little bit," she said. "A lot a bit."

"Of both?" He reached for her and pulled her closer and started kissing her along her neck.

"Well, let's put first things first," she said. "After all, it seems we have some unfinished business to attend to."

"Ooooh." Spencer's lips grazed hers. "I absolutely love unfinished business." He nibbled on her earlobe. "It's my favorite kind." He pressed himself up against her so she knew exactly what sort of work he had in mind.

"So, by business, then, you mean monkey business?" She pressed his lips open with her tongue, stroking along his teeth till he widened his mouth so their tongues could meet.

"I'm not monkeying around, if that's what you're asking." His fingers reached for the hem of her sweaterdress and he quickly skimmed it up and over her head. He let out a long, low whistle as he checked her out in a sexy pair of panties that tied at each hip and a sheer push-up bra that put her nipples on display. Throw in the silver sandals and she knew he was a happy man.

Georgie certainly had no idea that this was where she'd end up tonight—she didn't even expect to see Spencer at the party that wasn't a party—but she was sure glad she'd put on her most hopeful bra and panties. Hopeful because while she hadn't expected anyone, especially not Spencer, to see them on her, she knew any self-respecting man would go dry at the mouth if he did have the chance to see her dressed—or undressed—like this. Hoorah that she happened to luck into wearing her favorite silk undies rather than the gray grannies she could've donned, particularly because they had better fit her mood at the beginning of the evening.

Georgie struck a pose, thrusting her breasts toward him and cocking her hip in his direction. "You like?"

Spencer placed a hand on each breast, weighing them in his hands, then leaned forward and dragged his tongue along the fabric that outlined her taut nipple.

"I love." He deftly flicked the front hook of her bra, allowing her breasts to spill free of the cups. "And I love this even more."

He plucked one taut nipple between his fingers as his lips encircled the other one.

"Not as much as I love that." She moaned and pulled him toward her. She could hardly believe her good luck, considering how despondent she'd been earlier in the day.

He bathed her nipple with his tongue and she could sense it deep in her pelvis. It made her want more. It made her want him. Inside her. Now.

She grabbed his belt buckle and unfastened it, making quick work of the button and zipper as well, scooching his pants down like they were on fire. She pulled his sweater over his head and nodded toward the carpet.

"You." She pointed downward. "There."

"I like a woman who takes charge."

"That's me: large and in charge." She took a look at the bulge she couldn't help but admire. "Then again, you're looking pretty large yourself, big boy." She gave him a wink. "I like the mankinis, by the way."

"I considered myself on notice after your tightie-whitie tirade."

Georgie gave his shoulders a gentle shove and he helped himself down to the ground.

"Tirade?" she said, licking her lips. "I'll show you a tirade."

She knelt down and leaned over him as she shimmied his underwear down, then smiled. "Now this I could get used to." She dipped her head toward his hardened cock, stuck out her tongue, and drew a long swipe along the length of it. "Mmmm…"

"Georgie, baby, you're killing me." Spencer thrust his hips toward her as she took him into her mouth and sucked hard. He moaned when she grabbed his balls. "I'm not gonna last if you keep this up. I need to be in you. Now."

"Your wish is my command." She slipped her panties off and straddled his hips. Settling herself over him, she slid herself onto his swollen cock. She fixed her eyes on his as she ground her pelvis against him, circling her hips as she alternated rubbing herself on him and lifting her hips. Each time her pussy grabbed him and pulled him in, she gasped at the zings of pleasure it sent arcing through her pelvis.

Spencer guided her hips to help her lift and thrust, increasing the pace as she leaned forward so that he could catch her nipple in his mouth and suck hard. That was all it took to send Georgie over the edge as her pelvis spasmed around his cock, milking a climax from him as she pulsed on him. She collapsed on top of him, panting as she caught her breath.

Spencer rolled her onto her side so they faced each other.

"If you ask me," he said, twirling her hair in his fingers, "that was definitely worth a dead surfboard."

"Or two." She poked him in the ribs.

"Maybe even three or four."

They laughed as they cuddled on the carpet and fell asleep in each other's arms.

Chapter Twenty-Five

SPENCER glanced around Georgie's living room, marveling at the amount of Christmas decorations she'd managed to put up in such a short time.

"Did you own all of these? Or buy out the store?"

She grinned. "A little of both." She pointed to the huge tree in the corner, overlooking the ocean view. "I particularly like that touch, thanks to you."

He'd shown up a few days before Christmas with the tree and all the accoutrements, and they spent the evening decorating it together.

"It looks pretty good there, doesn't it?" He squeezed her hand.

"Almost as good as you look sitting here."

"Yeah, well, I know I'm not Bruiser, but…"

"You know that Bruiser chewed up two of my throw pillows while I was at work one day?"

"No!"

"Seriously, I came home, and it looked as if they'd been murdered. The stuffing carnage was over the top."

"Something about you and the death of inanimate objects." He grinned.

"Speaking of murdering prized possessions," she said, reaching for a package in a large gift bag she'd stashed behind the tree. "I was particularly glad that Bruiser didn't get his canines on this, which I have been saving for you."

"Is this what I think it is?"

She knit her brows. "You know about this?"

He pursed his lips. "Maybe a little bit. I don't know all the details, only that you had worked on something for me."

"Awww, man! Can't a girl keep a secret around here?"

"Consider it a good thing. Had Noah not told me about this, maybe I'd still be stuck on the idea of refusing to let anyone in. Even someone as kind and thoughtful and beautiful as you."

She smiled. "You think I'm beautiful?"

He nodded. "And kind and thoughtful. Those count too, you know."

"I know. Even more so." She handed him the gift. "Go ahead, open it."

He pulled out the quilt and had to stand up to hold it up all the way. "Holy cow—this is for me?"

She nodded. "You like it?"

"Are you kidding? I love it." He gave her a huge hug. "I, of all people, can truly appreciate what a labor of love this was to make. Even if you didn't know me, let alone love me. But I know it came from your huge and generous heart, so thank you, Georgie."

Tears filled her eyes. "Oh, no you don't," Spencer said, pointing at her eyes. "Don't you even think about it. There are to be no tears today. Instead, let's go over each panel of the quilt and see what you put in there."

He managed to distract her enough as he pointed to each one. "Ah, I have a special fondness for the octopus—how did you know that? They're such clever creatures. Have you ever watched them escape from things? They're amazing."

"Yes, they're brilliant. I can never eat them for that reason."

"There's a crab—been bitten plenty by them. Jellyfish, I'm not a fan but love him on the quilt. Seahorse—very cool. Turtles—the best. Stingrays—sometimes when we're waiting for a wave, they hang out with us. There's a surfboard with a cross marked RIP. May Petie rest in peace—"

"In my living room."

"Indeed. In fact I'm going to set my coffee cup on him right now. Oh look, there's a quilted shark—so far, I've managed to avoid them in the flesh, thank goodness. But I did laugh that day when you pointed out how lucky I was that you, rather than a shark, killed my board, which would have gotten me too."

She laughed. "Yeah and let's hope you don't exact revenge by killing the quilt in return."

"Come to think of it... If anything ever does happen to it, we could always repurpose it to something like cocktail napkins, maybe placemats."

She whacked him on the butt playfully. "From now on, no more hurting our things or each other. Deal?"

He nodded, pulling Georgie into his arms. "Deal. And for good measure, we can seal that with a kiss."

Thank you so much for reading *Falling for Mr. Maybe!* I hope you enjoyed it! If so, please help others find this book:

1. Help other people find this book by writing a review.

2. Sign up for my new releases email so you can find out about the next book as soon as it's available and get fun giveaways.
http://eepurl.com/baaewn

3. Like my Facebook page.
www.facebook.com/jennygardinerbooks

And I love to hear from readers! Let me know what you think about my books! You can write to me at jenny@jennygardiner.net, and visit me on the web at www.jennygardiner.net.

Keep reading for a sample from Falling for Mr. No Way in Hell, the next book in the Falling for Mr. Wrong series.

Falling

For

Mr. No Way in Hell

by Jenny Gardiner

Chapter One

LACY Caldwell secured her long, tawny hair into a loose side braid, pulled her goggles over her bright green eyes, then tugged on the iridescent teal mermaid tail that had, like it or not, become an appendage she'd gotten oddly attached to over the past year. Since last January, Lacy had been supplementing her income to pay for grad school by working as a mermaid at a cheesy roadside tiki bar in the small town of Verity Beach in North Carolina's Outer Banks.

At first she simply took the job because it was a job to be had. She'd never aspired to be a freak attraction to tourists looking for a good laugh while getting drunk over too many beers. But then she surprised herself by finding out she kinda loved both the job and the quirky group of people who she worked alongside at the Mermaid's Purse, too.

This included 87-year old Edna Dingleheimer, who'd been pounding out customers' favorite tunes on the electric keyboard four nights a week since the year John Kennedy was assassinated. Despite her one-of-a-kind appearance (bleached-blond beehive hairdo, Coke bottle-thick eyeglasses, knuckles knobbed with arthritis, dressed in a grass skirt over a pair of blue jeans), Edna's presence always took second fiddle to the main attraction: two mermaids who each night dallied in a swimming pool on the other side of a large picture window that overlooked the dark, dank bar of the Mermaid's Purse.

Sometimes Lacy could relate to how a stripper must feel, having leering eyes laser-focused on you for sometimes hours at a time. Even though she was, for all intents and purposes, far more dressed than a stripper. That said, the coconut shell bra wasn't exactly a turtle neck, and she had large enough breasts that they couldn't help but spill out a little bit from the tiny confines of those hard cups.

At first she'd felt self-conscious in her low-cut tail and coconut bikini top, but soon she realized it was sort of fun to get paid (and earn some pretty generous tips) to just flipper around a swimming pool for several hours a night. Since the pool was indoors, they weren't exposed to the elements, which was a huge plus. The biggest downside was sheer boredom: you could only do so much in a mermaid tail—a few underwater flips here, a handful of turns there, a couple of tail slaps with whatever other mermaid was on duty that night, and maybe send some seductive bubble kisses to the people at the bar, and then you had to get creative. Thank goodness she had to surface for air every twenty seconds or so, just for the change of scenery.

Often Lacy stuck around after work to chat with her co-workers. She adored the owner, Vera Cosmopolous, a seventy-something Greek American woman who made it her life's goal to fatten Lacy up, even though Lacy felt plenty fattened enough already, thanks.

"Here," Vera said, sliding a plate with grilled pita and baba ganoush, an eggplant and tahini dip, toward Lacy, who had to admit she was starved after swimming around in the pool for four hours. "This will be good for you and will help you get over that stupid man."

The stupid man she was referring to was her now ex-boyfriend, Billy Crapple. Yes, that was his name, deservedly so. Although Billy "What a Complete Pile of" Crapple was what she chose to call him nowadays. Lacy had devoted the past two years of her life to building a relationship with Billy, only to find out he'd been seeing not one, not two, but three different women at the same time. Three-timing Lacy. When she found that out—based on a phone call from one of the suspicious three-fers, accusing *her* of being the other woman, of all things—she kicked him to the curb, vowing to steer clear from men for the foreseeable future. From here on out, she was devoting herself to finishing up her degree and stockpiling money as a mermaid.

It was a good life. Or good enough, albeit a teensy bit lonely. Currently the biggest stressor in her world was that she had to attend the engagement party of her friend Carly, whose fiancé Jimmy was good friends with Billy. And the last thing Lacy wanted to do was show up dateless with him there.

"I tell you what you need, honey," Vera said as she helped herself to the pita bread she'd proffered to Lacy. Her electric green nail polish practically glowed in the dim light of the bar as she pointed at her mermaid employee who'd become like a daughter to he. "You need to bring a man with you and show that crappy Billy Crapple you never looked back once he was in your rearview mirror."

Lacy sighed. "Yeah sure. Great idea. But who might you suggest?" She looked around the empty bar. "I mean I could bring Stan with me—" she nodded toward a man twice her age with a bushy moustache and a wife at home, "but that wouldn't work on many levels."

They both laughed at the idea. Stan just scowled at them.

"Can't you think of any man who might go, even as a pity date?"

Lacy rolled her eyes. Just what she wanted to be: a pity date. Even though that's precisely what she needed to find.

"I dunno," she said. "I mean there's this nice guy I've chatted with at the gym. He was next to me in yoga last week, and I've seen him at the other end of the room in boxing class every now and then."

Vera shook her head. "Just as long as you didn't see him in ballet class, I say go for it."

"Like go for it as in, approach the guy whose name I don't even know, and say, 'uh, hey. I'm sort of a loser and can't find a date and I really need one badly to taunt my cheater ex-boyfriend and, well, we *did* do yoga together so it's almost as if we knew one another'?"

Vera waved her hand, dismissing the cynical suggestion. "It's as good an approach as any. Unless you want to put an ad in the paper."

"No one puts ads in the paper anymore."

Vera shrugged. "Oh excuse me. Then you can put a notice in Craigslist and I'll hope and pray you aren't murdered in your sleep." She clasped the cross dangling from her neck.

"Fine, I get your drift. I should just lose the shame and ask this guy. Even though I'm likely to see him every damned day at the gym, which will be perpetually humiliating if and when he turns me down."

Vera frowned. "Humiliating is when you're left at the altar with a bouquet of tea roses and no fiancé. I speak from experience."

It always saddened Lacy that Vera never did marry after that episode. Instead she made the bar her life and family, and now here she should be retired and enjoying life, but with no one to share it with, she just keeps on working.

"You do know that guilt trip isn't going to work on me, lady?" Lacy kissed Vera on the cheek.

Only it actually did work, every damned time she used that ploy. Each time Lacy thought about being alone and in her seventies, it just about prompted her to start looking for someone before she became old and lonely. Couple that with the need to prove to Billy that she'd long since moved on meant that she was indeed going to muster up the courage to ask her yoga buddy to be her date. Even if it killed her.

Chapter Two

CAMERON Sanders ran his fingers through his thick, wavy, dark hair, then wiped the sweat from his brow with one of those lousy, rough gym towels that felt like sandpaper on your skin. He knew he'd been hanging at the gym too much when he started to give a care about the texture of sweat towels. This is what happens when you're a down-on-your-luck artist making diddly squat painting caricatures of various tourists wandering around on the boardwalk.

It wasn't as if he wanted to be a professional kitsch artist, but man, it was hard making a living selling his real paintings. It was such a mercurial business, art was. And now that the gallery he'd been featured in had shut down, he was back to practically selling shit out of the trunk of his car, which was so not how Leonardo da Vinci did it. Of course Leonardo didn't even have a car.

Not that he was Leonardo. Or Michelangelo, for that matter. Or even whomever that person was who made the famous painting of the dogs playing poker. Perhaps he should have been doing commercial work like that and he'd not have so much free time to exercise at the gym for hours at a time.

"Hi," he heard a voice say. "You mind if I join you?"

He looked to his right and saw no one on the machine next to him so he turned to the left and saw that pretty girl he kept seeing in yoga class—the one he dared set his mat next to last time in the hopes she'd notice him. She didn't.

He nodded. "Go right ahead, be my guest." He extended an arm in welcome, as if he controlled who did and did not get to use the StairMaster next to his.

He didn't want to creep on her but he'd noticed her several times over the past month or so and it had occurred to him that if only he had a steady income and a career he could crow about, he'd have loved to ask her out on a date. But shy of a veritable overnight miracle, nothing in his life was going to change in the next, oh, forever, which meant he'd better tuck away such fantasies until he might some day be able to employ them.

He stuck his earbuds in and returned to watching last night's episode of The Bachelor, which he only watched because, well, who wouldn't want twenty gorgeous women fawning all over you while you drink to your heart's content and go on awesome vacations? This was the closest he was gonna get to the fantasy.

A few minutes later he felt a tap on his shoulder. He looked over to see the woman with the deep emerald-green eyes, so soothing and damp they reminded him of a cool pine forest in the summertime. Last time her hair was in a high ponytail but this time it was braided down her back. Either way it made him think how amazing it would be to have a firm grip on that hair of hers as he watched her mouth wrapping slowly around his cock. Which was jumping the gun a bit, since he hadn't even mustered up the courage to introduce himself, let alone invite her on a date. Nor would he, not with his depleting bank account and failing artistic career.

He glanced over at the woman who was sort of waving and using some sign language to communicate with him. He removed an ear bud.

She smiled. "Oh, god, I'm so sorry to bother you, but I just noticed you were watching The Bachelor and I totally missed it last night and wanted to watch it now but I forgot my earbuds and is there any chance you'd share one of yours with me? These things are so boring otherwise with nothing to watch."

He shrugged. Couldn't hurt to give her one—as long as she could keep pace with him on the StairMaster. And she looked plenty fit enough to do that. In fact with those arms of hers it looked like she could kick his ass if need be and right hook him into the next century. And that ass of hers was so perfectly shaped, just right to cup his hands around. And those legs. Well, shit, it didn't say much about him that all he could do was look at the woman and think how many different ways he might like to fuck her. Although wasn't that how every guy was? Nothing wrong with dreaming.

He handed her his left earbud and they started climbing again and for the next twenty minutes just climbed their stairs to nowhere together while indulging in someone else's fantasy world without actually being in it. It was all very meta.

Cameron was about ready to bail on the stair-climbing but every once in a while he got a great sidelong glimpse of her ass and that motivated him to keep on keeping on, at least for a few more minutes. Finally she tapped him on his shoulder and offered up the earbud. It made him feel a little sad that the moment was drawing to a close.

"Hey," she said as her fingers pressed the earbud into the palm of his hand. "Thanks so much for sharing. I really appreciate it."

He slowed down his machine till it came to a halt, then wiped his face again. "Sure thing," he said, taking a swig of water. "I was honored to share them with you."

She grinned. "Honored? Sheesh. I never knew it could be such a good thing for me to mooch gym supplies from someone. I'll have to get into the habit of that more often."

They stood facing each other behind their machines, dabbing off sweat and catching their breath.

"That thing about kills me," she said, placing her hand on her hip as she pointed a thumb at the StairMaster.

"Right? I feel like everyone else in here isn't getting nearly the workout we are."

She extended her hand. "Hi. I'm Lacy. Lacy Caldwell."

He slid his palm to hers. "Cameron Sanders. You can also call me Cam."

"It's great to finally meet you," she said. "I know we've been in a few of the same classes together. I think you were next to me at Vinyasa yoga the other day, right? And maybe boxing too?"

He nodded. "And don't forget Body Pump."

They laughed.

"Clearly we have shared interests," she said, glancing at her watch.

She shook her head. "No, not at all. I just have a class in an hour and wanted to be sure I had time to shower."

Well, crap. Now he's going to be obsessed with thoughts of her in the shower for the rest of the day.

"What a shame," he said. "I was going to see if you'd like to go grab some coffee."

She arched her brow. "Huh. Yeah, sorry, I don't have time for that now." She pinched her lips with her fingers as an idea emerged. "Though please forgive me if you think this is weird, but I have another idea that might be fun. Bear with me." She held up her finger. "So, I'm only suggesting this because we're practically family now that we've shared earbuds and all." She grinned. He loved her smile, those white teeth all nice and straight and perfect.

"You've got my attention," Cameron said, wrinkling his brow. "And I'm really hoping you aren't asking me to join you to, say, visit your husband in jail."

She shook her head and held up her hand with a barren ring finger. "Oh, trust me. No husband. No way, no how." She dusted off her hands to get rid of that thought.

"I have to admit that's a bit of a relief." More than a bit, now that he'd put himself out there by asking her out for coffee.

"In that case, I hope you don't think this is really weird of me." She scuffed the toe of her sneakers along the carpeted gym floor as she stared downward.

"The longer you wait the bigger chance I'm going to conjure up some really bizarre scenario in my head and then that will be weirder still."

She shook out her hands as if she was trying to wake up a sleeping limb. "Okay, here goes." She sucked in a breath. "So, you see, I have to go to this party and this ex-boyfriend who is a total jerk is going to be there and I really just need to take someone—anyone—as long as he's male and has a pulse, though it doesn't hurt if he's good-looking, so that I don't look like a dateless loser, and I was wondering if maybe you'd be that person perhaps?"

Cameron lifted an eyebrow. He was completely amused by her half-cocked invitation. He shook his head as if clearing his brain.

"So let me get this straight. You need a prop. To make your ex-boyfriend jealous. And I'm as a good a one as any.

It's unclear as to whether I fall into the good-looking prop category or if I'm just the man with a pulse." He lifted his brows in question.

She squinted her eyes. "That didn't come out so well, did it?"

He laughed and waved his hand. "Not to worry. I've got a tough hide, so I didn't take it personally."

"I'm sorry. I didn't mean to be rude."

"It wasn't rude at all. Just sort of funny. In a peculiar way."

"Peculiar as in you're going to humor me and be my date to Carly and Jimmy's engagement party so that Billy Crapple can see that I've moved on?"

He cocked his head. "Have you moved on?"

She ski-sloped her brow. "From Billy Crapple? Hell yeah. Believe me, there was no love lost there. I was happy to be rid of him. I just don't want him to think I can't land a man and I need him back or something."

He took a swig from his water bottle. "Well that's the silliest thing I've heard of. Clearly," his gaze slowly scanned her from head to toe, "You could land any man you set your sights on."

She pointed at her red, sweaty face, strands of hair clinging to her forehead. "Yeah, especially right about now, all smelly and sweaty."

"I can assure you no man would be turned off by a sweaty woman." He grinned. "Quite the contrary, in fact." He didn't want to scare her off with being too suggestive so he diverted the conversation. "But in answer to your question, I'd love to be your pulse."

She jumped up and clapped her hands. "Oh goody! And honestly, you're way more than a pulse—you are one hundred percent good-looking prop material."

Cameron had never been more thrilled to be used by a woman in his life.

Falling for Mr. No Way in Hell

coming March 13, 2018.

About the Author

Jenny Gardiner is the author of #1 Kindle Bestseller *Slim to None* and the award-winning novel *Sleeping with Ward Cleaver*. Her latest works are the *It's Reigning Men* series, the *Royal Romeos* series and her new *Falling for Mr. Wrong* series, beginning with *Falling for Mr. Wrong.* She also published the memoir *Winging It: A Memoir of Caring for a Vengeful Parrot Who's Determined to Kill Me,* now re-titled *Bite Me: a Parrot, a Family and a Whole Lot of Flesh Wounds*; the novels *Anywhere but Here*; *Where the Heart Is*; the essay collection *Naked Man on Main Street*, and *Accidentally on Purpose* and *Compromising Positions* (writing as Erin Delany); and is a contributor to the humorous dog anthology *I'm Not the Biggest Bitch in This Relationship*.

Her work has been found in Ladies Home Journal, the Washington Post, Marie-Claire.com, and on NPR's Day to Day. She was also a columnist for Charlottesville's Daily Progress for over a decade, and is the Volunteer Coordinator for the Virginia Film Festival.

She has worked as a professional photographer, an orthodontic assistant (learning quite readily that she was not cut out for a career in polyester), a waitress (probably her highest-paying job), a TV reporter, a pre-obituary writer, as well as a publicist to a United States Senator (where she first learned to write fiction). She's photographed Prince Charles (and her assistant husband got him to chuckle!), Elizabeth Taylor, and the president of Uganda. She and her family and menagerie of pets now live a less exotic life in Virginia.

Visit Jenny at her website at www.jennygardiner.net where you can sign up for her newsletter, visit her blog, or find her on Facebook and Twitter. And every blue moon she'll post adorable pictures of her pets on Instagram as @thejennygardiner.